Praise for *Always a Wanderer*

"*Always a Wanderer* is a powerful, inspiring tale that proves not all who wander are lost."

—Sabrina York,
New York Times and *USA Today* bestselling author

"Readers will be captivated by the enchanting and mysterious world of The Irish Traveller series."

—Kate SeRine,
National Readers' Choice Award-winning author

—

Praise for *Once a Gypsy*

"A haunting and fresh voice in paranormal romance. Be prepared for Danica Winters to ensnare you in her dark and seductive world."

— Cecy Robson, author of the Weird Girls series
and 2016 Double-Nominated RITA® Finalist

"Winters' sweet opener to her Irish Traveller series bodes well for future titles."

—*Booklist*

ALWAYS A
WANDERER

the IRISH TRAVELLER series
BOOK 2

DANICA WINTERS

DIVERSIONBOOKS

Diversion Books
A Division of Diversion Publishing Corp.
443 Park Avenue South, Suite 1008
New York, New York 10016
www.DiversionBooks.com

For more information, email info@diversionbooks.com

First Diversion Books edition June 2017.
Print ISBN: 978-1-68230-848-6
eBook ISBN: 978-1-68230-847-9

To Mac—
May we always wander together.

The only business of the head in the world is to
bow a ceaseless obeisance to the heart.

—William Butler Yeats,
Letter to Frederick J. Gregg, 1886

CHAPTER ONE

It seemed that people who were like her, people with the gift, were always searching for the truths of the universe while their bodies struggled with reality. Helena O'Driscoll refused to be like the rest of them, the ones who forgot they were standing in the middle of a room, only remembering they were still alive when the lights were off and everyone else had gone home. She couldn't let herself get lost in the mist, the veil that obscured life at Adare Manor—regardless of how badly she sometimes wanted to disappear.

The wind stroked the few leaves that clung to the trees, tickling them until they whispered their secrets into the evening air, only to be garbled by this place's mysteries. The breeze carried the scent of the River Maigue, earthy and round, rich with the heady aroma of an Irish fall. She pulled the smell deep into her lungs, hoping for a brief moment that it would fill her with the same promise of renewal, but as she exhaled, she realized the truth—her new reality had become her cage. It trapped her in a way she had never thought possible, a way that went against everything she'd ever been taught and the blood in her veins—she was imprisoned by her heart.

Graham stepped beside her and put his hand to her lower back, his touch hot on her skin. "Are you okay, lass?" he asked with a smile. His full pink lips were the lips she had kissed a hundred times, but each time she noticed them as of late, it was as if they belonged to a stranger.

"Aye, I'm fine," she answered, with a smile that mimicked his—the same tight lines and forced edges.

She could see her lie register in his eyes, but he didn't push further. She stared at his strong features and the way his dark brown eyes seemed to have lightened the moment they had left Adare's grounds. He was so very handsome, and it made her heartbeat quicken as she thought about reaching up and running her thumb over the stubble on his jaw. Somehow it felt *off* to touch him like that now.

Graham slipped his hand into hers, but his fingers were tight and she let go as he opened the doors to the Clonshire Equestrian Center and followed her inside. It was sweet of him, really, to try and take her out when there was so much to do at the manor to get ready for the new hospital's grand opening.

A man on a piebald gelding rode up to them. The horse's hooves struck the soft dirt with heavy thumps as the man pulled the animal to a stop. "'Ello, so glad to have you here, Mr. Kelly. How's your da?"

The man had an indiscernible accent, and as he sat back in the saddle, he ran his hand through his thick curls of blond hair. He reminded her of the models on the covers of the array of horse lovers' magazines that always seemed to adorn the tables of the sitting rooms around the manor.

"Mr. Shane is right as rain," Graham said, his voice as tight as his smile. He glanced over at her, checking her expression.

She knew what he was thinking. The last thing—or person—either of them wanted to talk about was his step-father. Thanks to differing opinions about the hospital, the manor, and life in general, they had endured little but constant fighting and bickering with Mr. Shane over the last few months, and his name left them both with a sour taste in their mouths.

"Glad to hear it," the man on the horse answered. "It's been a while since he's graced us with his presence. His mare, Glenda, is missing 'im." He motioned toward the corridor, where the stables could be found. "No one can handle her as well as your step da; she always seems to want to please 'im."

"That horse sounds just like my mother," Graham whispered, so low that only she could hear.

Helena bristled at the thought. She couldn't understand how anyone who really knew Mr. Shane could fall for him. He might come off to some as ever so likable, but it was nothing more than a businessman's show—all for the money and prestige—and when it was stripped away and he stood bare, he was nothing more than pound signs.

"Are you Ms. Helena, ma'am?" the blond man asked.

She tried not to notice the way he stared at her for a moment too long. He shifted in the saddle as though he were making room for her to climb up and ride away with him.

Truth be told, he looked like the type of man who could have any woman he wanted, but she had no interest in adding her name to the list of women he'd taken for a ride. She glanced over at Graham, but he didn't seem to have noticed the man's unspoken dialogue.

She gave the man a polite smile. "Aye, and you'd be?"

"I'm Neill Morgan, the riding instructor here at Clonshire Equestrian Center. It's mighty fine to meet you, ma'am. I've been hearing much about ye."

She shouldn't have been surprised that she had been talked about even outside the manor. She was a freak—a gypsy who had strayed too far from the path of her culture, and she was an outsider amongst the upper echelons.

"Nothin' of merit, I'm sure," she said under her breath.

"What was that, my lady?"

She shook her head and waved him off. "Nothin', just sayin' there ain't no reason for you to be callin' me my lady. Just call me Helena."

"Aye, as you wish." He smiled, and his gaze moved down her as though he were stacking her against the ladies she was now expected to emulate.

He would be sorely disappointed in her if he thought she could be anyone other than the Traveller woman she had been raised to become.

"What kind of riding do you like to do, Ms. Helena?" Neill continued.

She had grown up around horses. When she had been young, Da had always taken them to both the Appleby and Ballinasloe horse fairs. It had been one of the family's few annual traditions. She and the other children loved it— that was, until Da had been carted away to the clink and their family fell apart. Now, like so much else, the thing that had once made her who she was had become nothing more than a fading memory.

"I grew up around Vanners. Always loved the thrill of the race, they are wicked fast beasts," she said, trying to ignore the feelings of nostalgia that swept through her.

"Racing, eh?" Neill said with a chuckle. "I guess I ain't surprised…You bein' who you be and all."

"What do you mean by that?" Graham's head rose at the man's innocuous words; perhaps he had misunderstood the tone.

"Ah, nothin', sir. I just be sayin' it's nice to meet someone who fits into this place as well as I do—you know, about as well as a culchie comin' up to Dublin."

From the looks of him, Neill fit in just fine, with the thick blond locks that framed his face and the jawline that could have been chiseled out of marble. The only thing that gave the man away as *other* was his thick accent.

As much as he wanted to make her think their lives resembled each other's, he wasn't anything like her. Regardless of his background, he belonged here—surrounded by the elite women of high society, who likely fawned and coyly batted their eyelashes until they found themselves alone with him in the recesses of the stable.

"Do you got any Vanners here?" she asked, more than aware that they would have been just as out of place in the equestrian center as she was.

Neill shook his head, but he smiled as he must have realized that she had asked the question not out curiosity but out of spite. "'Fraid not. I've been pushing to diversify our breeds, but right now we concentrate on Irish sport horses, like this guy here." He ran his hand down the gelding's neck. "How about we do a little riding, aye?"

She glanced over to Graham. He was checking his mobile, likely thanks to the seemingly hundreds of e-mails he got each day asking him questions about the manor and its employees. There was always something that needed his attention—normally more than her.

He looked up at her and caught her gaze. "Sorry, lass." He turned off the screen and slipped the thing into his pocket, as though he were as annoyed by it as she was.

"Aye. Everything okay at the manor?"

He nodded. "They're having problems with the…" He paused as he looked at Neill. "The new *venture*," he said, carefully avoiding the word "hospital." "They can't seem to get everyone settled."

"Was there another runner?" Her thoughts went to Herb and the near tragedy they had faced earlier in the year.

Graham's face grew pinched. "Let's just say they are missing us—or more accurately—you."

There must have been someone who needed her gift, the power of her healing touch. She stretched her fingers and drew them into a tight ball. Her body was tired, but she couldn't deny anyone the help they needed and, in truth, she wanted to get away from Neill as quickly as possible.

She turned on her heel and moved toward the door. "Let's go back."

Graham grabbed her hand. "No. The staff can handle everything for a few hours. This is our time. We've been working so hard; we need a wee break. Everything will be there when we get back."

He was right, but that didn't make her feel better about

staying. If she'd learned anything in her last few months at the manor, it was that she was really good at only one thing—helping those whose bodies needed healing. Everything else, like love and relationships…well, those were things that, no matter how hard she tried, she always failed to master.

Graham slipped his fingers between hers. "Let's have a go." He motioned toward Neill. "Are the horses ready?"

Neill nodded, but his features tightened as he glanced down at Helena's and Graham's entwined fingers.

For a moment, she thought about pulling away from Graham, but instead she squeezed his hand tighter. They had their problems, and they were still trying to fix what was awry in their relationship, but that didn't mean that she was ready for another man—another gorger, no less—to make a move. Not that he was making a move—maybe the way he kept looking at her, and the way he smiled when she caught his eye, maybe they were nothing more than attempts to make a friend in a world where he felt he didn't belong.

Regardless, she stepped closer to Graham's side.

Neill nudged his piebald gelding around and moved toward the stables. The horse pinned his ears back, annoyed at the man's prodding, but Neill forced the horse forward with a press of his foot. The gelding sidestepped, fighting the command, and threw his head up with an irritated nicker.

"Ya need to get down," Helena called.

"He's just throwing a right fit. He needs to know he can't get away with it," Neill answered, pulling the horse's head straight.

She could feel the energy as it radiated from the horse.

It buzzed through the air, building as the animal's muscles rippled and flexed beneath the man in the saddle. The horse didn't like the man on his back, or the way he pressed him forward when he wasn't ready.

Neill raised his hand, ready to strike the horse.

The horse looked back, the whites of his eyes showing as he watched Neill's hand rise into the air.

"Don't. No," Helena called, but it was too late.

Neill moved to strike, and the horse lurched, catching him off balance. Seizing the moment, the horse pitched forward. Neill swayed in the saddle as he tried to hold on to the animal's body with his thighs.

The gelding sprinted ahead, forcing Neill back in the saddle. He struggled, but as he moved, his actions threw the horse's balance off and the animal tripped.

Helena watched in horror as their bodies spun through the air. Neill's eyes were wide, and his mouth hung open. A shrill whoop of fear and surprise escaped him.

His body hit the ground with a heavy thump. Dust filled the air, shrouding the man in a blanket of fine silt, as though he were being buried alive.

She gasped as the gelding flipped, his legs flailing as he struggled in vain to right himself. No matter how hard the beast fought, he could do nothing to stop his descent, and he came crashing down atop Neill.

There was a flurry of motion, the animal's legs thrashing as he panicked and kicked at the air. Catching himself, the horse rolled over the body beneath him with a creak of leather and the sickening crunch of bone.

The sound—the echo of what was undoubtedly the man's death—was something Helena would never forget.

CHAPTER TWO

The blood dripped from Neill's chin, falling to the ground and forming a shallow pool. His chest was concave where the saddle had crushed his ribs. His arms had already taken on a sickening, mottled purple-gray color.

Helena rushed to the man's side and laid her hands on his chest. His energy seeped into her fingers, weak and leaking out just like the blood that poured from his wounds. The constant thump that marked life was faint as he clung to the land of the living.

"It's all right, Neill...you'll be all right...you'll be okay," she said, though every cell of her being told her he was far from fine.

He looked up at her with icy blue eyes, desperate.

"Help him..." Graham urged.

"Ring the medics." She laid her hands on Neill's crushed chest. Her fingers brushed over the oily surface of a bone that had broken through his skin and torn into what had once been his crisp white shirt.

The horse stumbled as he regained his balance, his eyes white with fear. As Helena looked at him, he tossed his head and squealed in pain.

"Take the horse to the stables. The animal needs to be checked out."

Graham took the horse's reins and ran his hands down the skittish animal's neck. The horse pulled, but as Graham spoke he started to calm, and Graham was able to slowly coax him toward the stables.

Neill's chest shifted under her fingers, pulling Helena's attention back to his wrecked body. Her powers had grown stronger since coming to the manor, but looking at the state of him, she wasn't sure how much help she could actually be. Mending a bone here and there was far different than putting together a man who looked more like Humpty Dumpty after his great fall.

She grounded herself, pushing her fingers deep into the soft dirt as Ayre had been teaching her. "Powers of the earth, be with me. Bridge the gap between the world of the living and the land of the dead. Fill the space with your energy. Help me to help those in need," she whispered. "*A libha sarog. A karkn lugil. A dha ogaks moniker, d'umiik a libha nalks, dha karkn fhas, dha lugil kuldrum.*" She repeated the old Cant prayer in English—she needed all the power she could get. "The blood is red. The flesh has pain. In the old one's name let the blood dry, the flesh grow, the pain sleep."

A wave of energy ran up from the ground, pooling in her core like she was a battery being recharged. She sighed, letting the power fill her. Hopefully this would work. Hopefully she could put the man back together again.

Then again, if she did…he would know her secret.

She stopped for a moment, and the flow of energy ceased.

What would happen if he found out who she was? What she could do? He wasn't like them. He wasn't a supernatural. If she healed him, he would have the knowledge and power to strike down everything she and Graham had been working toward.

Was this man, and this one man's life, worth putting their kind and the people they were trying to save at risk?

What would happen if the nonsupernatural world found out there was another side—a side they would not understand?

At first, the public would possibly be excited, welcoming even, but the ethics of the situation would make it nearly impossible. A future where her kind was no longer a secret would be difficult to navigate. Who would she save, and when? She could barely understand her power now. Put her on display for the entire world, and many would think she was a fraud, and those who didn't would come to hate her when she couldn't give them something they wanted. Regardless of the powers she held, she would never have the power to please everyone.

And then what would become of her life at the manor? Mr. Shane would be furious.

She tried to hold back the thoughts of angry mobs bursting through the doors and threatening people's lives. It hadn't been that many years since the end of the Troubles. During those days, homes had been burned and bombs had ripped through the countryside—all thanks to self-justified hate and misunderstanding. Irish history was full of bloodshed carried out for a variety of reasons; if the truth of the other side—the supernatural side—came to light, it would most certainly end in social discord and a bloodbath.

She shuddered and the energy spilled from her fingers, falling back into the ground.

She couldn't let her life be dictated by fear. She couldn't stop herself from helping a person in need because she was terrified of a future that might never come. Yet the needs of one couldn't outweigh the needs of many.

She clutched at the dirt, letting the tiny pieces of stone dig into her palms until it hurt. The pain pulled her back as she stared into Neill's blue eyes.

She was given this gift to share, not mete out like it was under ration.

The energy moved back up her arms, warming her from the inside.

Laying one hand on Neill's forehead, she gently placed the other on his abdomen. His pain radiated from him, and she forced the energy from her hands, concentrating on the pain and encircling it with her power, pulling it from him. She started at his core and his lungs. Focusing on his breath, she spread wisps of energy through the punctured tissues, knitting them together.

He gasped for air, and she sat back. Foam bubbled from his lips, dripping down the sides of his face, and she rolled him onto his side. Pain coursed into her hands, but it was muted.

That was enough healing. He would live. His heart would continue to beat.

Nature could mend the rest.

She heard the sounds of footsteps running through the soft dirt of the arena.

"Is he okay?" a woman asked from the center.

Helena sat back, wiping off the dirt on the legs of her pants. "Aye, he'll be okay. I hope," she added.

"What in the bloody hell happened?" the woman gave her a look filled with contempt, almost as if she thought Helena was somehow responsible for the horse rolling on the man.

Thankfully, Graham came running. "The medics are on their way. They should be here any minute." He looked down at Neill and the woman at his side and then sent Helena a questioning glance.

"I think he'll be okay. There are a few broken bones, but nothin' major," Helena said, letting the unspoken truth fill the space between them.

Graham nodded in understanding.

"No. Don't…" Neill moaned.

"What?" Graham asked, kneeling down at the man's side.

"Don't. No hospital. No."

"You daft bastards." The woman turned to Graham. "First you get him hurt and then you go on and call the authorities? He'll be deported, so it is."

"What are ya talkin' about?" Helena asked.

The woman stared at her. "Neill," she started, "Neill has a past. The authorities be lookin' for him. If he goes to the hospital, they'll cart him away. He'll be in the clink—or worse—in no time. We have to sneak him away before the medics get here."

Helena remembered her da standing outside Limerick prison, gaunt and tired, aged beyond his years.

They could take Neill to the Adare hospital and keep

him out of the clink. He wasn't the right *kind*, but if they kept him separate, maybe they could get him treatment—treatment that didn't expose Helena's gifts.

"Graham," she said, her tone questioning.

He chewed on his lip, and she knew what he was thinking. If they took Neill to the hospital and he saw what they were doing there, the kind of people who enlisted their services, they would never be able to explain the place—or why they had it on the manor's grounds.

If she had learned anything over the last year, it was that nothing good ever came of lies—the truth always had a way of coming out. If they wanted to stay completely safe, and remain under society's radar, it would be best to leave the man to pay the consequences of his decisions. Yet if they did nothing, Neill's freedom would be stripped away—just like Da's had been.

She looked down at Neill. He had curled his broken body into a fetal position, and the motion pulled at her heartstrings. Regardless of the man's sins, he was someone's child…someone's lover…maybe even someone's father.

Once again, he was hers to save—or to condemn.

"Can ya lift him?" she asked, turning to Graham and putting her hand on his arm.

He glanced at her fingers as if they were the key to everything. With one simple touch, her will would be done.

"Are you sure? You know the risks." Graham put his hand on hers, stroking her fingers.

Maybe he did love her. Maybe they hadn't lost their connection. Maybe time had simply muted it. Yet their relationship didn't feel the same as it once had. The first time he had touched her, she had nearly melted under his fingertips. Now her reaction was simply a slow burn, a desire to be near him, to have him touch her again. The raging inferno had cooled.

"If we give him enough drugs, he won't notice a thing. We just need to get him the help he needs. We're the reason he's hurt," Helena said, responding to Graham's unspoken concerns.

The woman at Neill's side looked up with a grimace on her face. "I knew you two eejits were having me on. Neill's too good a rider for something like this to happen. What in the hell did you do?" She stood up and charged at Helena, so they stood nose to nose.

"Do ya think I wanted him to get hurt? That I wanted this?" Helena said, shocked by the woman's anger and resentment toward her.

"I saw the way you were looking at him. You're nothing but a gypsy whore." The woman's spittle sprayed her cheek. "What happened? Did he turn you down?"

Helena guppied for a moment, her mouth opening and closing as the woman's verbal blows struck her. Did she really think Helena had tried to hurt Neill because she was an unrepentant whore, or worse—in the woman's mind—a gypsy?

"Stop. Right. There. You don't have a right to talk to her like that." Graham pushed between them. "Helena didn't do anything. In fact, she tried to help your…What is he? Your boyfriend?"

The woman looked away.

Graham shook his head. "Ach. You have this all arseways, woman. Helena here told your *friend* to get off the damned horse. He was being an arse and didn't listen. He was the one at fault, not her."

She felt vindicated by Graham's reproach of the woman, and special because he felt strongly enough for her to stop the woman's accusation dead. Yet, at the same time, she resented it. She could stand up for herself. She'd lost so much of her identity—she couldn't lose the strength that made her who she was. But now wasn't the time or the place to tell him how she felt.

The woman moved to speak, but Graham stopped her with a wave of his hand. "Save it. Whatever you have to say, I don't want to hear it."

"Regardless of your *gypsy's* role, she admitted you two are the reason Neill's hurt. You have to help him," the woman commanded.

Graham sighed and looked over at Helena.

She gave him a reaffirming nod. The woman could say what she wanted about her and the kind of woman she was, but when push came to shove, Helena valued freedom above all other things. If she could save Neill from a fate like Da's, it had to be done.

"We're going to get him out of here." Graham motioned toward the door and his white Mercedes parked just outside.

"Where you be takin' him?" the woman asked, her tone like that of a petulant teenage girl, so much so that it reminded Helena of her sister Rionna. Most times, she missed her sister, but at the sound of the woman's words, she was reminded of all the reasons to be thankful Rionna was no longer her burden.

Graham's face tightened. "Somewhere he will be safe."

Even if my kind won't be.

"You stay here," he told the woman. "Take care of the horse. He needs your attention."

"What about Neill?" the woman countered. "You can't expect me to just go along with this, and you not tellin' me where he'll be."

"Don't worry, as long as he's with us, he'll be fine." Graham turned away before they could be barraged with any more questions.

Even though Helena should have believed him and bought into his promise, she couldn't. Nothing was going to be fine—she could feel it in her bones.

• • •

Something was wrong with Helena. Her aura was a dark red, Graham noted, the color of stress and indecision. Perhaps it was just because of the man in the backseat, huddled in a hay-scented horse blanket they had found lying in the tack room.

For so many reasons, it had been a hard decision to help the man, but none made it harder than the fact that Neill had seemed a little too friendly when it came to Helena. It would have been only too easy to leave him lying there to face whatever the world was going to bring his way. But this wasn't really about Neill. This was about Helena and her need to save people.

He glanced over to where she sat in the passenger seat. She was looking back at Neill, and as she said something to the suffering man, her dark hair caught the light, making it look like it carried bits of copper in its strands. As if she could sense him watching her, she turned and gave him a slight, almost questioning smile.

"Ya all right?" she asked.

He nodded.

Everything was far from all right, but now wasn't the time to bring up the feelings, the masked moments, or the secrets they shared.

He pulled the car to a stop at the Adare hospital, a former fortress that rested just off the bank of the River Maigue on the corner of the Adare estate. Over the last century, the place had fallen into ill repair, its stony walls crumbling and collapsing in upon themselves, leaving sentinels as a reminder of the many battles fought there. However, over the last few months, they had rebuilt the place. It had been a mammoth undertaking. They had strengthened everything, from the walls to the water lines to the roofing, even as the bond between the two of them weakened.

Sure, she had made the choice to stay here, at this place, with him. They had told one another they loved each other, but the moment her mother and sister disappeared and she made the choice to stay, everything changed. It was like she was an entirely different person. She was more reserved and serious. She poured herself into their work, but it was almost as if he had caused a bit of her to disappear—and he hated himself for it.

He eased Neill out of the car, careful to avoid bumping the man's chest. Helena's touch had knit some of the skin over the bones, but from the dark bruising on Neill's arm and wrist, Graham doubted she had been able to fix everything that had been broken.

Neill moaned, the sound rife with agony at the sudden movement.

"You'll be fine," Helena offered.

Graham looked at her. She was giving off a light rainbow aura, her normal glow, the glow of a healer.

"Where…where are we?" Neill said between pained breaths as they walked to the hospital's front doors.

"It's…uh…" Graham stammered, trying to come up with the right words.

"It's a pop-up clinic. The manor wanted to do somethin' for the locals. You're a right lucky man, Neill. Who knows where the clinic'll be next week," Helena said, covering up for his stammering.

Neill glanced at Helena, his features tight with pain, hiding anything that would tell Graham whether or not the man actually believed the story they were trying to sell.

Graham opened the door to the infirmary. The place wasn't even officially open—the ceremony wasn't for a few days—yet it already carried the pungent aroma of antiseptic and commodes. The scent reminded him of tired flesh and thinly stretched minds.

He thought of the former infirmary under the manor, which had always smelled like a dungeon—dank and earthy. Perhaps, as bad as this place smelled, it was better. In the dungeon, even though the patients were still alive, it was as if they were already buried.

The new infirmary was going to be a place where he and Helena could carry out real healing—instead of tucking the patients, people like them, away in an early grave.

He moved Neill to the nearest open chair in the lobby and helped him sit down. At the desk sat a receptionist dressed in a crisp, pinstriped suit, similar to those worn by the manor staff.

"Hello, sir." The receptionist looked at Neill. She closed her eyes and drew in the scent of the man. "Sir, the man... he's not..." She frowned as she looked to Graham.

"He's not *like the rest of our patients*. I'm aware," he said, stressing the words. "However, it was an emergency. Is one of the private rooms open?"

The former infirmary had been ward style, open beds, like something out of an earlier century, but thanks to the money they had raised, they had been able to afford to create several private rooms in addition to the four-person wards. After what had happened with Herb and his mother, rooms in which patients could be heavily monitored seemed to have been a long time coming.

"I'll need to talk to the charge nurse," the receptionist said, motioning to the nurses' station that sat on the other side of the locked doors behind her. She stood and disappeared into the main infirmary.

He walked over to Neill. "Mind if I take a look at what we're gonna be working with?"

Neill shook his head.

He pulled at Neill's shirt, lifting the man away from Helena as Neill grunted in pain.

"Ach...Gentle," Neill grumbled.

"Aye," Graham said. Helena moved closer, offering with a tip of her hand to help him, but he waved her off. "I got him."

He carefully pulled up the edge of Neill's shirt. His

stomach was covered in lines of bruises where the saddle and his clothing must have pressed into his flesh. There was a red patch on his chest that looked as though it was freshly healed skin—almost as if a rib had protruded and, thanks to Helena's gift, had been fixed.

He sucked in a breath as he looked at her work. Without a doubt, she had saved the man's life.

She really was amazing. And it was no wonder Neill wanted to lean on her. Whether he realized it or not, she was his savior.

If only their relationship were as easy to fix as flesh and bone.

The receptionist came back out, followed by two nurses, one of whom was pushing a wheelchair.

"We'll take him back. The doctor is waiting," the blond nurse said with a gentle smile. They lifted Neill and helped him into the wheelchair.

"Aye, good. Let us know what they find," Helena said with a nod.

The nurses and the receptionist pushed the broken man through the doors and out of sight.

"We need to talk," Graham said, but as the words fell from his lips and a look of terror filled Helena's face, he wished he hadn't spoken.

"What's wrong?"

"Nothing," he said, trying to make his voice light. "I just think we haven't gotten a chance to really spend time together. We've been so busy lately, with everything going on around this place."

"We couldn't even get our date right, could we?" she said with a little laugh.

It sounded so good, hearing her laugh. It had been a long time since he could remember her making that sound. He'd missed it.

The front door swung open, hitting the wall with a metallic thump.

"What do you think you're doing?" Mr. Shane threw the door shut behind him. "Did you really think you were going to get away with this?"

They looked at one another. Had Mr. Shane heard about the intruder in their midst? How had he found out so quickly?

"I can't believe you went behind my back and let a non-super anywhere near the hospital. Could you two be more stupid?"

"Who called you?" Graham asked, going toe-to-toe with his angry stepfather.

"It doesn't matter who called me. You know how much I disagreed with you moving the infirmary, and now, before the official ceremony to celebrate the opening of the place, you are putting us all in danger. What if someone finds out about this? There are people out there, hate groups, who are looking for any reason to come after us. They are salivating, eager to get their teeth into any supernaturals they find. Do I need to remind you of the consequences that would arise if the manor were associated with something like this? Every life here could be at risk if they find out what we're doing. Think about what the press would make of it. It could cost me everything."

Graham cringed at the word "me." Everything was always about the business and Mr. Shane's own needs. It was never about the people.

"You know as well as I do that this place needed to happen. I'm not having this argument with you again, John," Graham said, using his stepfather's first name in an effort to equalize the fight.

His stepfather grimaced. "That's not what I was saying, Graham. Though I disagreed, I let you move forward because you promised that you would keep this place quiet. And yet, you are attempting to screw us all. You have no concept of the position you are putting not only me in but everyone else as well. You are more than aware there are hate groups out there—groups that would love nothing more than to find a place like this...full of people like you and your brother...and burn it to the ground."

"You're overreacting," Graham said, continuing his argument.

Mr. Shane smiled, the gesture slow and dangerous. "No. I'm not. And before things get to that point, and someone gets hurt, I think it's best if I shut you down."

CHAPTER THREE

Graham continued arguing as Mr. Shane got into his car and slammed the door in his face. It hurt Helena to be forced to stand idly by.

Mr. Shane wouldn't dare shut them down. They had poured so much time, money, and effort into the place. Just getting the money necessary had taken an extraordinary amount of work, since the manor and the man holding its purse strings had refused to support their dream, and all donations had to come through families who knew their secrets. Mr. Shane had been fighting them every step of the way. Maybe Helena shouldn't have been surprised that he would do it again now, when the last pieces were so close to falling into place.

There were times when she wondered if Mr. Shane's goal in life was simply to make Graham's as difficult as possible. It was hard to understand their mercurial relationship. One minute they would be in a mutually agreed upon period of peace, but if there was even the slightest disagreement, things would rapidly deteriorate and Mr. Shane would turn against him—just as he did now.

It was more than frustrating, and she felt for Graham. He worked so hard to make his dreams happen, but was constantly thwarted by the man above him. If it hadn't been for his brother Danny's still-tenuous health, she was certain he would have left this place long ago.

"Graham," she said, putting her hand on his shoulder. "Don't worry about him. He's just got a bee in his bonnet. He'll come to his senses."

Graham turned to her, and his face was twisted with rage. "He's a damn eejit. How can he think that he has the power to just shut us down? Sure, he owns the land, but goddamn it, we're the ones...This is ours." He motioned toward the hospital. "He has no right. I won't let him."

"As long as we can keep gettin' funded without his help, we can keep goin'." Even as the words fell from her lips, she was aware of the futility of them. She and Graham were in control of the events in their lives and the future of the hospital about as much as a bird was in control of the direction of the wind. All they could do for now was be carried by it, not fight against it. Some things were too powerful. And sometimes the best thing to do was wait to fly until the squall died down.

"Mr. Shane will cool off. We just need to make sure Neill won't whisper a word of this place to anyone who shouldn't know. We need to keep everyone safe." The need for safety was the only thing she could agree with Mr. Shane on.

A whisper of guilt rose up from her belly. She had caused this. She had known the risk, but she had acted with her heart once again. Her heart was an impulsive thing, a thing she thought she could control, but when she was forced to make a difficult decision—it always pulled her further from logic and deeper into emotion. Damn her heart.

Graham took hold of her waist and pulled her closer to him, so they were face to face and his breath warmed her skin. Was he going to kiss her? It had been such a long time. The thought made her chest ache with sadness and longing—and a touch of loneliness.

Hopefully her heart wouldn't lead her astray once again.

Graham reached up and pushed a stray hair behind her ear, and he let his fingers graze over the line of her chin. "I know things have been hard between us. I'm sorry."

His words were weighted with emotion, but it wasn't enough to fix all that was wrong between them. She wanted him to kiss her, but he pulled back and dropped his hands from her waist.

"Let's get out of here and do something just for us. Something fun," he said. "No horses. Nothing dangerous. Just me and you, and maybe we can get Mary to pack us up a bite to eat."

The thought of Mary Margaret made the chasm in her grow a little wider. When Helena had come to the manor, it had been as a simple cook, chopping and mincing and talking to the kitchen maven. When she'd made the choice to stay and work with Graham at the hospital, she knew she would have to give up her position in the kitchen, but like so many of the other aspects of her life she'd left behind, she missed it.

Life had been so much easier before. And, as much as it surprised her, the days she had spent looking after the children and moving around the countryside caring for her mam—in many ways, they had been easier too. At least she'd known what the day would bring. And there wasn't the constant threat of death if her gift failed; there wasn't the pressure of pleasing others, or fixing the world—rather, it was a life spent one day at a time. It had been a life of simple pleasures and moments of silence in a world that changed too fast.

"Helena?" Graham asked, pulling her back from her thoughts.

"Ya know what?" She glanced down at her mobile. By this time Angel would be home with Liam, and Da would be back from his work as a groundskeeper. Right now she needed nothing more than to be with her family. "I'm gonna head back to the cottage."

Graham's face fell, like she had just thrown salt into Mr. Shane's freshly laid lashes.

"It's just that…" she started, trying to lessen the sting.

"No. I get it," he said with a wave of his hand. "Nothing's going right today. Maybe it's better if we call this one and just rest before the grand opening."

A wave of relief moved over her. Reality had proven to be so different than what she'd imagined six months ago—when she'd come here with idealistic thoughts of living a life in which only love and Graham mattered. Maybe that was exactly what had happened to Angel when she'd married the gorger. Maybe her heart had told her love was enough, but when life got in the way and she was standing alone when all she wanted to do was stand together, that idealism disappeared, and she was left with only the harsh light of reality.

"Do you want a ride?" Graham asked, motioning toward his Mercedes.

She shook her head. "Nah, I need to stretch my legs." She gave his hand a light, quick squeeze. "Ring me later."

She leaned up on her tiptoes and gave him a quick peck on the cheek. He smelled of the hospital's antiseptic mixed with the earthy scent of hay from the equestrian center.

If nothing else, he had tried. He had tried to make the day special for them. It was just too bad that the world kept getting in the way.

• • •

The manor was abuzz with life as the staff decorated for fall. They had placed little wreaths of orange leaves and red berries across the tables in the halls, and garlands of red and orange leaves over the doorways. The place was warm, ready to start the celebrations that preceded Christmas and the winter equinox, but it carried chilly whispers of what could come to those who were unprepared for the days ahead.

Graham made his way up the double-winder staircase and toward John's office. He couldn't leave things as they were. The man had no right to threaten them. Not when they had worked so hard for so long. It was just another of his stepfather's power plays—a way to manipulate them into doing whatever dance he had in mind.

If John really wanted to shut them down, he could have done it long before now. There had to be something else going on.

Graham knocked on the heavy wooden door of the

man's office, and the sound echoed back at him. "John, we need to talk."

There was no answer.

"John," he repeated.

Mr. Shane could have been any number of places, but it was rare that he wasn't in his office at this time of day. Then again, after their argument, maybe he had decided to take a break.

Graham reached down and pulled out his mobile. He'd missed three phone calls, and there was a text message from the main nurses' station at the hospital:

We need you here. Incident with new patient.

Mr. Shane, and the conversation they needed to have, could wait. He needed to extinguish the biggest fire first. He thought about calling the hospital and finding out what was wrong, but instead he stuffed the mobile back into his pocket. His head ached with the stresses of the day, yet he was no closer to finding the answers he needed. Maybe it was selfish, but he needed these minutes to reorient himself and find a few moments of quiet.

The darkness of night pressed down, and the lights cast long, skeletal shadows through the small car park in front of the hospital. A deep autumn chill filled the air, and he tried to ignore its bite as he made his way inside.

The charge nurse stood in the lobby waiting for him, her hair pinned up into a honeycomb bun and her face tight with stress. "What took you so long?"

It had taken him less than ten minutes to get from the manor back to the hospital, and in truth he wished it had taken even longer. "What are you talking about?"

"We've been waiting." She motioned for him to follow her into the back. "I…rather, we…have a problem."

He followed her to Neill's private hospital room. John stood beside the door. He was so pale that his skin had taken on a green tone. John opened his mouth to speak, but then he stopped and looked down at the floor.

"What the feck happened?" Graham strode to the door and pushed it open.

There, hanging from the ceiling, was Neill. His face was bloated and blue, and there was a sickening purple tint around his bloodshot eyes—it was the face of a corpse.

CHAPTER FOUR

Helena stared at the cottage's kitchen wall. Its white paint was peeled back, as if it didn't want to be stuck in this place. The walls pressed in on her, and an edge of panic rose up from her core.

On evenings like this, when she had so much on her mind, she couldn't help wishing she were back in the world of trailer living—a world where she could just walk outside and sit beside the campfire and stare at the flames. It was the best way she had ever found to get back to her center—to the core of who she was, where she could reconnect with her true self.

She glanced out the window. Outside stood row after row of headstones, each leading up to the Holy Trinity Abbey Church. In her old life, she had been surrounded by change, progress, and forward movement. Yet here, she was surrounded by varying states of decay.

"Helena, can ya give me a hand in here with the boys?

Liam's being a right wily thing," her sister called from down the hall.

Helena made her way toward the bathroom, where Angel was trying to cajole her son into staying in the bath. There was the sound of splashing and Liam's squeal. He kicked as Angel tried to pour a cup of water over his head to wash the shampoo out of his hair. He burbled and sputtered as the water ran over his face.

"Seriously, lad, it's just a wee bit of water. We don't need the theatrics."

Helena and Angel's younger brother, Gavin, was sitting on the toilet, fiddling with a plastic boat and singing a song as he waited for his turn.

"Look at Gav," Angel said, trying to divert her son's attention. "He's being such a good lad. Can you be like your uncle?" The stress in her voice reminded Helena of their mam.

She stood staring at her sister for a moment. More than anything, she didn't want the two of them to slip into the roles they had been taught as young children. She couldn't stand the thought of either of them turning into their alcoholic, narcissistic, and bitter mam.

Liam grabbed the cup of water and let it go, spilling water all the way down Angel's shirt and into her lap.

"Gawd, boy. What were ya thinking? Now I'm going to have to change my clothes. Don't ya got a brain in that head?"

Helena reached over and touched Angel's shoulder. Her sister was stressed. She needed a break. "It's okay. It's just a bit o' water. Go change. I got the lads."

"Aye." Angel stood up and wiped a wet hand over her

forehead, leaving water on her skin. "Ma'aths, gra. They're gettin' on my last nerve."

"Have a cup of tea. I'll be along."

Angel gave her an acknowledging nod as she made her way to the kitchen.

As Helena washed the last bits of slick soap out of Liam's hair, her mind wandered. A year ago she had been doing basically the same thing—taking care of kids. At that time, she had wanted nothing more than to finish up her schooling, go to university, and follow her dreams. Had she made a mistake by giving it all up?

She leaned in and sniffed the top of Liam's head. He was too old to carry the baby scent, but he still smelled of youth and innocence—of a life full of decisions and promises. What she would give to be unencumbered again. To be naïve to the fact that with every path taken there were many left behind.

Were there ever any right or easy answers? Any correct decisions?

She tried to imagine where her life would be if she had gone to university. No doubt she would have been sitting in some classroom somewhere, trying to learn the ins and outs of anatomy or biology. She would be struggling through the required classes in nursing and learning the basics of mathematics and science. She'd likely be getting the side-eye from the gorgers in her classroom.

Helena couldn't forget the time in secondary school when she had been called to the front of the class for yet another absence earlier in the week—Mam had had one of her trips down the bottle, and Helena had been forced to stay home and take care of Gavin, who at the time couldn't have been more than a few months old. She was humiliated, standing there in front of her entire class, her dirty knees poking out from under the edge of her uniform—a reminder that she'd crawled out of the trailer that morning so she could get out unnoticed and unpunished by Mam. No one knew. No one *could* know. Nothing good would have come of the authorities finding out about her home life.

Yet the worst part wasn't standing there blemished by her mam's choices and her own rebellion, but rather the look of derision the redhead in the front row gave her. It wasn't even so much a look as an outright judgmental assault on everything that Helena was and stood for. And it didn't end there. When Helena was finally ordered to sit, the girl loudly proclaimed a piece of human trash like her had no place amongst them—and she was disappointed Helena hadn't permanently disappeared from their lives.

She could have lived with the girl's disdain; she was hardly the first person to look down her nose at Helena. But the support the redhead garnered—the collective nods and sneers—broke her heart.

In that moment it was hard to remind herself that she and her family weren't trash. It wasn't until she excused herself and made her way to the bathrooms, where she could really look at herself, that she could remember who she was—she and her family were Travellers. Pavee, to be exact. They'd never be understood or accepted, and they weren't the kind who required others' validation to know their own worth. There was much to be proud of—deeply held traditions about the importance of family, hard work, and the ability to embrace change.

Even with that knowledge, facing bigotry at the university, day in and day out, would have been just like her days in secondary school. The only difference would have been that there were more people to despise her. At least at the manor, for the most part, she was accepted.

Sure, there were still a few who gave her a wide berth in the hallways, or wouldn't speak to her, but being with Graham provided her and her cultural background with a certain level of legitimacy. Or maybe it was just that everyone had been forced to accept that she and her family were going to become a part of the manor, and their lives.

No matter where she went, or what she did, she would never be completely welcome. She would never fit in. She'd never be perfect.

She sat back and let Liam play in the water for a moment. Was that the battle she had been fighting within herself all this time? Had she been trying to fit everyone else's vision for her? Had she been trying to be everyone's perfect everything?

Angel walked into the room as Helena wrapped Liam in a towel.

"Thanks for takin' 'im. I dunno, sometimes I just get so…"

"Frustrated?" Helena said, finishing her sister's sentence. "It's all right, lass. We all got our moments."

What she really wanted to say was that she feared they were following in their mam's footsteps, but she resisted the urge. No doubt Angel felt the same as she did—the pressure to be more and to rise above.

Angel nodded, but her gaze fell to the mug of steaming tea she held in her hands.

"Maybe ya need to get out of the house. You've been cooped up in here for the last few months. Maybe it's time for something different—a change, ya know?"

Angel looked at her like she'd lost her mind. "Who would watch the children? The last thing I need is for Duncan to find somethin' he can use against me. This divorce has been hard enough—if he thinks he can get Liam from me, I'm sure he'll try. I can't give him no grounds. I can't lose my son." She set her cup on the white bathroom counter and moved to dry Liam's hair. She gazed at him like he was a fragile dust mote, and if she moved too fast or tried to grasp him too hard, he would slip through her fingers and disappear.

Helena understood that fear. In a way, it was how she had felt about Graham when they first started dating.

"Don't be controlled by your fear of Duncan. He won't get Liam. You're a right wonderful mam. He doesn't have a snowball's chance in hell of getting the court to side with him for custody. Liam has only ever had you."

"We are who we are, gra. You know as well as I do that a judge would take one look at me and hand Liam over to the gorger. He's stable. He has a job."

Helena cringed as the echoes of her fears fell from her sister's lips. "We are stable. We are settled now." The walls seemed to move in a little closer around her. "And we can get ya a job. We talked about it before, but maybe now it's time for ya to come work in the kitchens…or if ya wanted somethin' else, maybe I could talk to Graham and get ya in. Ya could wait tables."

Angel's eyebrow rose skeptically as she waved down at her clothes. She had on the same tube top she'd worn the first week she moved into their little cottage, and her jean cutoffs were so tattered that the ends of the pockets hung lower than the hem. "I bet they would just love this look in the Oak Room. I'd fit right in with the ladies in their fancy hats."

"You can change your clothes." Helena felt like a bit of a fraud; fitting in at the manor wasn't as simple as getting a new wardrobe.

"That ain't all that's gonna stop me, ya know it. Ya think they won't hear the way I talk? And you and I both know the second someone tries to go smartin' off at me…I'll be fired my first week."

"Ya don't have to work with the public. There's any number of jobs, Angel."

"And what about the kids?" She motioned to the boys.

"There's daycare for Liam, and Gavin's in school. Between Da, you, and me, we can take care of them. We can make this work—as long as gettin' a job at the manor's something you want."

Angel nibbled at her bottom lip as she led Liam and Gavin out of the bathroom and toward the bedroom they all shared. She looked around the tiny room, packed with a medley of brightly colored secondhand toy swords and robots, stacks of hand-me-down clothes in laundry baskets with no place to go, and the two bunk beds that had come with the cottage.

"Aye, it would be okay. I mean, it would be right helpful if I set about earnin' some money. Maybe we could, ya know, look for a place of our own." She waved at the room around them. "I dunno about ya, but this ain't my idea of paradise."

Helena wasn't sure if her sister was including her in the plan to leave or not, but she hated to ask.

Her home life was so much calmer, and Helena had grown to enjoy life in the little cottage. She hated to think of what would become of their dwindling family if her sister and Liam left. The thought of this blip in time ending made her ache with loneliness.

"Besides," Angel said, "you got enough on your plate to worry about. I think it's time I start thinking about my future. With me taggin' along, you'll never be welcome at another campsite."

"I ain't plannin' on going back to a campsite anytime soon. And if they got a problem with ya, they can take it up with me." Helena smiled. "As for now, don't worry about movin'. Just do what ya need to do. Go on ahead and save up and plan for the future, but I'm happy to have ya here."

"But wouldn't you like your privacy? I know things are heatin' up between you and Graham."

Was her sister really that oblivious to things outside the home? Graham and Helena hadn't been heating up for months.

"Don't worry about us," Helena said, tucking Gavin in bed beside Liam with a quick kiss on the head. "Love ya, lad."

Angel kissed Liam and she and Helena made their way out of the room to the box of a kitchen and sat at their rented table. Her sister thumped down into one of the green vinyl chairs and stared at the mug of tea in her hands. She still looked wrapped up in her thoughts of getting out of this place.

In many ways, Angel wasn't wrong about needing to

move. They were still living on the church's grounds and at a cheaper rate than they should have been. It bothered Da, so much so that he'd been home less and less, as summer turned into fall and he let his work consume him. When Helena saw him, he was always working around the church grounds, mowing the grass or fixing a broken pew. He had made it clear that it was his way of repaying the church for their kindness—but from the tight look on his face whenever he came home to rest, she wondered if he felt the strain of their arrangement as well.

"Do ya really think we would be better off if I quit and we moved along?" Helena asked.

Angel stood up and poured herself another cup of tea and one for Helena before sitting down across from her. Angel took a long drink of the hot liquid. In fact, it was such a long drink that Helena wondered how she wasn't burning her tongue. Finally, she slowly lowered her cup and tapped her fingers on its sides.

"Gra, I know how hard this must be on ya. This world's hard. Our world is hard. And bringing the two together is…well, it's damn near impossible. I failed. But I'm here because I'm not giving up. I want my family. Wherever we go. Whatever we do. We will make it, so long as we always remember to love one another." Angel stopped moving her fingers. "And that goes for you and Graham too. I know it's not easy to stay close when your worlds are always pullin' ya apart. In the end, that's what happened to Duncan and me. I couldn't bridge the gap. But again…that don't mean you won't be able to. Graham's a right good man. He's good for you. Look at all that you've done together. Ya built the hospital. You're helpin' not just people now, but far into the future."

Helena thought of Mr. Shane and his threat and her mistake with Neill. The future—including the hospital's—wasn't guaranteed.

• • •

The hospital was bustling as nurses rushed past him and patients cried out from their rooms for care. Graham had always thought he had nerves of steel, but listening to their moans as he looked up at the corpse made him shudder.

Why would Neill have killed himself? Did it have something to do with his criminal past? Or had Neill not done this to himself? Was it possible they had a murderer in their midst?

Graham had so many questions going through his mind as he stared down at his mobile and tried to decide whether or not to tell Helena. She had saved the man's life, only to have him die at the hospital. It had taken a toll on her—using her magic always wore her down—and the worst part was that none of it made sense.

He looked over at the man. Neill's eyes were open and unseeing, and the little capillaries around his pupils had burst, sending starbursts of crimson throughout the bulging orbs. Graham had seen death, but the man's eyes—his gape of the tortured—forced him to look away.

"Cut him down," John said, motioning toward two of the male nurses who were standing just outside the room's door. "And I don't want anyone to speak of this."

He glanced down at his watch. "What time is the grand opening tomorrow?"

The last time he'd spoken to his stepfather, John had been threatening to shut them down, and now he was asking about their party for the opening? He couldn't be serious.

"Are you fecking kidding me, John?"

"The show must go on." His stepfather gave him a withering glance, but he didn't look away. "Why don't you and I step out for a bit? Let them clean up this mess." John looked to the nurses, who were readying to cut down the corpse. "Take the body down to the morgue. I'll have my people notify his family."

What in the hell was wrong with the man? First, he didn't want anyone to speak about it, but now he was going to notify Neill's family? And tell them what? That Neill had died at a hospital that wasn't supposed to exist? And what about the police? Last year, in the case of Chester's death in the manor's kitchen, they had called in the police and it caused turmoil for the whole manor, between the loss in revenue and the PR disaster the death became. A disaster they were just starting to overcome. John had been vocal about another event of its sort not happening again. Yet, here they were.

Graham followed John to an empty room at the end of the hallway—well out of earshot of the staff.

"You had no right calling me out in front of them," John said, shutting the door to the room behind them. "Regardless of what you think, you are not in control. You don't own the manor, this hospital, or the land that any of it resides on—I do."

"You and my mother."

John answered with a smug chuckle. "Are you going to call her, so she can come and defend you?"

Rage seeped through him. He'd always had a strained relationship with his stepfather, but he'd never wanted to punch him in the throat so badly.

"I don't need my mother's—or your—permission to speak my mind. I am the chair of this hospital, and as such I have a right to question and refuse to accept your bullshit."

"Mine? How about you take a look at yourself? I'm just trying to get you—and *my* hospital—out of the possibly catastrophic position you and your little gypsy queen just put us in."

John could speak of Graham and his position—but he had no right pulling Helena into this. She had done nothing wrong.

"Don't you fecking dare. She did the right thing in bringing the man here. She saved Neill's life and what could have been his future," he said, letting the acid roll off his tongue. "Yet we leave you alone with the man, and a decision you didn't agree with, and then the man ends up dead. I doubt it's just a coincidence."

"Are you accusing me of *murdering* him?" John's face pinched into a tight scowl. "You are more idiotic than that gypsy if you think I'd be so stupid as to put everything I love at risk because I didn't agree with you and your woman. There are a thousand ways I would have controlled that situation before I'd decide to have that man killed. I wouldn't stoop so low."

The way John spoke made every hair on the back of Graham's neck stand on end. "We both know that isn't true. If there is even a whisper of money involved, you will do whatever you need to get ahead. Even if it means selling your wife's—or your son's—soul."

John's jaw clenched, and Graham could hear the sound of him grinding his teeth with poorly contained rage.

"You think you're so fucking different than me. But you don't understand anything. Do you know how hard I've had to work to keep this manor afloat? Especially when we were starting out? How dare you judge me."

"You nearly killed the people who loved you the most. Was it worth it?"

His stepfather closed the distance between them and pressed his face so close that Graham could see the little black dots of the pores on his nose.

"You don't know what you're talking about," he said, spittle hitting Graham's cheeks.

Graham refused to step back. "You used them with the book. You thought the *Codex Gigas* would be the answer to all your money problems. Now, again, there is something, a man, who stands in the way of possibly making this hospital profitable—when there is money on the table, murder is far from being out of the question for a man like you. Right now, with all the pieces coming together to make this place profitable, you aren't going to let anyone stand in the way."

"What are you talking about? I didn't want this hospital in the first place. I've never been behind the project." John paused. "But if you run this business like you run your mouth...Hell, I won't even have to lift a finger to be afforded the pleasure of watching you fail."

"I won't fail. I *can't* fail. These people, those with abilities and their families, depend on this place. We're all they've got." Graham wiped the spittle from his face. "You may say you're not behind this, but you could have stopped it months ago if you really wanted to. Let's be honest with one another for once. You and I both know that you had us do the legwork and find the funds to build this place, and now you're just waiting to deposit the checks."

"You're talking out of your arse."

"No. You have a plan for this place. I know it. You know it. It's all about business. You want people to come here, get help—and pay for the service. You probably have a marketing plan in place to make sure their families stay in and around the manor grounds as well—don't you?"

John remained quiet.

"I fecking knew it! You just want to make money. You don't give a rat's arse about who it will help, or the good it will do the community."

John finally stepped back. "You and I both know that I was never keen on the idea of the infirmary in the basement. Yet, it had to be done. We had to get the care your mother and brother needed." He took a long breath. "I didn't see it as a business possibility then. I was a fool. All your work showed me that I had missed a profitable opportunity. There was a need. Now we can fill it." John spoke with a self-righteous and egotistical air. "And you would be smart to see it as a business venture as well—that is, rather than some philanthropic cause. Altruism is for those who can afford it. You certainly can't. You need to run it like it's any other clinic. Albeit you need to do it carefully. You really screwed things up with this Neill situation. You do realize we're going to have to pay off a number of people to make sure that his death is covered up in an adequate manner?"

So John had had no intention of telling the man's family—of course not. Everything he did was for show.

Then again, John wasn't wrong in some respects. They were going to have to cover up Neill's death.

"We can't just bury him and forget about it," Graham said. "If there's a killer in our midst, we need to figure out who it is. We can't have someone randomly murdering the people in the hospital."

John nearly rolled his eyes with exasperation. "First, you don't even know if it *was* a murder. For all we know, the man was just depressed. Whatever happened to him, it doesn't matter. We had a problem. It solved itself. There are better things we could be using our time for. Are you even ready for the grand opening?"

"Don't try to change the subject." Graham glanced down at John's well-manicured hands and couldn't help but wonder how dirty they really were. "If you're behind this, tell me now. Save me the legwork."

His stepfather laughed. "I already told you I didn't do it. No reason for it."

"Then why are you resisting? Why do you want to cover it up? Don't you care what happens to the rest of the people in this hospital?"

"Look, Graham, his death is inconsequential. Let's call it collateral damage in your soft opening. There's just a number of other things that need our—mostly *your*—attention. I doubt that this type of thing will continue happening."

"You seem very sure of that, John."

His stepfather shook his head as he walked to the door and put his hand on the handle. He turned back one more time. "You are a fool if you think following this one down the rabbit hole will end with anything less than disappointment and anger. You need to look at your opportunity costs. By wasting time investigating this meaningless death, you're giving up time that you could spend making money."

"Feck you and your money. I can't let this man's murder go unsolved. I will find out who is behind this—I have to keep those under my care safe." Hate roiled up from his core. "If I find out that you or one of your cronies was behind this man's death, I will make it my personal mission to bring you to the ground. I will take every last thing from you—including your precious manor."

CHAPTER FIVE

The morgue smelled of metallic refrigeration units and the tang of chemicals mixed with the stench of unfulfilled dreams. The odor was sickening, and Helena wanted nothing more than to get out. A grossing station was set up in the corner, and stainless steel doors lined the walls, while a steel autopsy table stood at the room's center. A scale hung over it, just waiting to be filled with lumps of flesh.

Death didn't scare her, but this place did. There was something so industrial and dehumanizing about it, like the people destined to find their way to this place were pieces of meat that needed tending, rather than beings who, only hours or days before, had been coursing with energy and life. It reminded her of a slaughterhouse.

"Are you okay?" Graham asked, putting his hand on her lower back. "Do you need to sit down?"

As he spoke, her body swayed slightly.

"Here," he said, taking her gently by the arm and leading her to a small white plastic chair that sat at the front of the room.

She sank into the reassuring safety of the chair.

"You don't have to be here. Giorgio and I can handle this." He motioned to the guard he'd called to meet them in the morgue.

Giorgio had once been a forensic pathologist and a member of the First Greek Raider/Paratrooper Brigade and had graciously agreed to come along and help them go over Neill's body to see if they could find any clues as to the cause of death. Giorgio was tall, so tall in fact that if he reached up he could have rested his palm on the ceiling with ease. He had broad shoulders and a neck that was just slightly wider than his head. It was almost as if whoever had designed him had put his head on as an afterthought.

Helena drew in a long breath, trying to ignore the stench of the place. "I'm better now."

"Are you sure, miss?" Giorgio frowned as he stared at her.

She quickly glanced away, afraid he would be able to see the guilt in her eyes.

Helena stood up and brushed off the legs of her pants, more out of habit than need. "I'm right as rain. Now, where's his body?"

"The morgue attendant said he was right over here," Giorgio said, pointing to the wall of steel doors.

She made a show of walking toward the row of refrigerated units in the wall—like they didn't frighten her, though as she neared she could barely make out the sound of the industrial fans over the thumping of her heartbeat in her ears.

Giorgio walked over to box fourteen and unclicked the handle. He glanced over at her one more time before opening the door and pulling out the long table where Neill lay.

His body was covered with a white sheet, and it reminded her of something off one of those crime shows she had often seen on the telly. She tried to tell herself it was just like the show in an attempt to distance herself from what lay under the sheet.

If there had been music, like in the show, it would have had some kind of dirge-like beat, low toned and slow. She started to hum the tune in her head. Graham looked at her and frowned, and she promptly stopped.

Giorgio handed them each a pair of blue nitrile gloves, and she pulled them on over her shaking hands.

She had to be strong. Not just for herself, but for Graham as well. Yet it was hard to feel strong when there was the nagging feeling that Neill was here because of her. If only she had left him to be tended by the medics, maybe he would have still been alive. It would have been better for him to end up in the hands of the authorities and set to be deported—at least then he might not have been lying on a cold table in a morgue.

Just like every other decision she had made, it was hard to tell herself it had been the right one.

Graham reached up and pulled the sheet down from Neill's face.

His bloodshot eyes were wide open, but they had started to take on the milky opaqueness of the dead. His blond hair was limp and lay in jagged angles over his forehead. Giorgio moved him, rolling him slightly as he inspected the body. Lividity had started to set in, and Neill's back had turned slightly gray thanks to the lack of circulation. Where his shoulders touched the table, blood had started to collect in dark patches under his skin.

She had to swallow back her feeling of sickness as she compared the vibrant man she had met to the decaying corpse in front of her.

"If you look here"—Giorgio pointed toward the bruising on Neill's neck—"this's definitely a ligature mark, and if you notice the broken capillaries in his eyes, those are both signs of strangulation."

"Aye, we found him hanging."

Giorgio looked up with a raised brow. "He was definitely strangled to death, but that don't mean he wasn't already dead when they strung him up."

The guard ran his finger over Neill's neck, inspecting the dark bruise that marred the man's skin, and then he moved lower, to Neill's arm. He picked up the right arm, which was slightly rigid but gave under his touch. He inspected the back of it, down to Neill's hand.

"See here? See how the flesh is open, and there's no clotting?" Giorgio pointed to a jagged cut over Neill's knuckles. "He hit someone at or near the time of his death. And he has defensive marks on the back of his arms." He lifted the arm so she could see the scratches on the back. "Marks that wouldn't have come from his accident."

"Ya think he tried to fight someone off, and they constructed a scene to cover it up?" Helena asked, trying to follow the man's train of thought.

Giorgio shrugged. "It's hard to know exactly how the man died, but you'd be best served if you didn't jump to any conclusions. In a case like this, you never know what you're gonna discover. Only one thing's for sure. This fellow didn't kill himself. Someone else was behind his death."

So many questions were running through her mind. If only the answers would come as easily. "No one knew where we were takin' him—at least not from the equestrian center or from his personal life. Whoever did this had to have been involved with the hospital. Who here thought they had so much to lose that it was worth taking a man's life?"

Graham had told her about his conversation with Mr. Shane, and though the man had insisted he hadn't been behind the killing, everything seemed to point in his direction. He was the only one who had any kind of motive. And, so far as she knew, no one in the hospital had even known Neill.

She tried to control her shaking hands. "Is it possible there's something else going on? Something we're missing? Who would do such a thing?"

Between staff, patients, and guests, there were about a hundred people who had been in and around the hospital at the time of the murder. There were no cameras, as their patients typically requested they not be videotaped, so any kind of investigation into Neill's death would be challenging.

"Whoever did this had to be someone big enough to overtake him. And then strong enough to lift him." Giorgio motioned toward the ceiling, like they were standing in the room Neill had been found hanging in.

Giorgio pulled the sheet up to Neill's thighs, exposing his tanned, hairy legs. They were the legs of a rider, toned and well-muscled after a lifetime spent gripping the back of a horse. On the inside of his right calf near his ankle was a brand similar to one that might be found on a horse's rump.

"He must have taken his job as a horse trainer very seriously…Or else this means somethin' else." Giorgio pointed at the strange marking.

The mark looked as though it had been on Neill's skin for some time. It was in the shape of a triangle, pointed at the top, but its bottom was open and a series of lines ran through its center. Helena had never seen anything quite like it.

Graham leaned in close, inspecting the mark. "I've seen that somewhere before." He took out his mobile and snapped a few pictures of the mark and the bruises on Neill's body. "But I couldn't tell you where."

Giorgio lifted the sheet, so he could look over the rest of Neill's body, and Helena turned away to keep from seeing the whole man. She felt silly looking away, but she couldn't bring herself to look upon his nakedness.

Graham gave a gentle cough, as if cluing Giorgio in.

"My apologies, miss," Giorgio said.

"It's fine," she said with a backward wave.

Graham slid his hand over her lower back, making her jump. "We're done. Nothing more to note."

"What are we gonna do with him? If any else sees him…they're going to want answers."

"We're going to have to bury him. The sooner the better. Mr. Shane is right about one thing—we don't want this blowing back on us," Graham said. "Giorgio, can you handle it sometime this afternoon? I have to meet my mother. In the meantime, I'll talk to the priest. I'm sure we can find a spot for him outside the main cemetery."

Giorgio nodded.

"What if they wanna have an autopsy done? If they ask that the body be exhumed?" she asked, shuddering at all the morbid thoughts and images that came to her mind.

Graham sighed. "We can get the medical examiner to write a report to cover it up in case anyone comes poking around. Just say that he died due to a horseback riding accident. Head injury. Easy enough."

"Why don't we have him cremated?" she asked. "Then there's no way...ya know."

"She's right," Giorgio said. "I'll have our staff take care of it. If you agree, sir, you can consider it done."

Graham answered with a stiff nod. "In the meantime, we need to find out who was behind this and why. The last thing we need is anyone else in this place getting hurt. If someone, a staff member or anyone associated with this hospital, is hurting people, we need to stop them. We can't risk losing everything we have worked so hard to attain."

All Helena could think about was Mr. Shane. She was sure he was behind this. And it was up to them to bring him down.

• • •

The manor was full of guests, and as Graham walked through the parlor, he was greeted with a slew of tilted caps and slight bows from those who had come to celebrate the hospital's opening—the only thanks he and Helena could be given within their world of secrets.

The secretary at the front desk smiled as she saw him

approaching with Helena at his side. "It's so lovely to see you both. Congratulations on the upcoming *events*," she said with a guilty smile. "Is everything ready, or is there anything I can do to assist you?" She gave Helena her warmest smile.

Helena had handled the morgue surprisingly well— that was, after her brief moment of light-headedness. He had wanted to make her leave, force her from the macabre scene, but he had no power to make her do anything she didn't want—her strength was one of the things he'd always been attracted to.

He couldn't help the grin that spread over his face as she smiled and her brown eyes lit up when she smiled. She was so beautiful. If only things were different between them.

The phone rang, and the secretary answered. After a moment of not speaking, she frowned and put the phone back in its cradle. "That was Mr. Shane," she said, her voice devoid of the energy that had been present only seconds before. "He says you're late. He's waiting for you in the study. You are to rush."

He glanced down at his watch. His mother's therapy wasn't for another ten minutes. John was just trying to be a pain in his arse—or rather, to intimidate him and make him look powerless in front of Helena again. Either way, he couldn't let John get to him. His mother had to come first.

"Thanks," he said to the secretary as he slipped his hand into Helena's.

She gripped his hand harder than she had in a long time. Her palm was damp. Was she nervous about touching him, or was it excitement? He looked down at the way her hand fit ever so perfectly in his, and as he looked up he caught her gaze and she smiled.

Yesterday it had been as if they were little more than strangers, but seemingly overnight something between them had shifted. It was as if they had gone back in time—to a time when things were easier between them.

He lifted their entwined fingers to his mouth and gave the back of her hand a long kiss.

"Oh, aren't you a sweet man?" the secretary said, pulling him back to the fact that they were still in public, and in the middle of the manor.

He looked to the secretary. "If you liked that, you are going to love this." He pulled Helena into his arms.

For a moment the world disappeared around them. There was only the feel of her lips on his, the flick of her tongue as it searched for his. His body awoke, quivering to life at the spontaneous display of affection. It felt so good, holding her in his arms, feeling her mouth move over his as she pushed for more, a deeper kiss…a deeper need…a deeper want.

Oh, Jaysus.

He pulled back and set her on her feet before his desire for her was visible to the entire manor staff. That was exactly what he didn't need to be known for.

Helena stumbled, and he caught her by the waist and held her. Her breath was quick and uneven, and there was a sheen of sweat on her forehead. Apparently she had enjoyed their kiss as much as he did.

"Your…your mam," Helena said, patting at the sweat on her brow. "We need to hurry. We don't need any more *issues.*" As she said the word "issues," her gaze drifted to his lips and a new wave of sweat seemed to rise on her skin.

He loved that he had made her feel that way, and though he didn't exactly mean to, he couldn't help but gloat internally. She wanted him—or at least her body did. As for the rest of her, only time would tell.

They made their way upstairs to the study. Books lined the walls of the room, kept private for the family and their guests' personal use. He couldn't remember the last time he had actually spent any real time in this room, and for a moment he wondered why John had continued to keep it off limits to the paying guests.

His mother, Rose, was sitting on the Victorian-style lounge, complete with pink, floral-printed fabric that seemed to fit the woman who rested upon it. Since May, she had started to gain a bit of weight, and her cheeks and face had taken on a healthy shape and color. Her hair, still gray, was now clean and coiffed in a perfect chignon. Her Chanel suit hugged her nicely, and if he hadn't known the trauma she'd experienced over the last few years of her life, she could almost have pulled off the illusion of normalcy. That was, until he looked into her eyes. As beautiful as she was, her eyes still carried the storms that tormented her soul.

The storms…the reason they were all here.

"Hello, sweetheart. Helena, so nice of you to come," his mother said, standing as they entered. Her tone was light, as flowery and fake as the couch she had risen from.

She could have saved herself the effort. Everyone in the room knew what she tried so hard to hide.

Helena gave her a quick kiss on each cheek, and Rose

turned to him. Her forced smile disappeared. "I keep trying to tell them this is all unnecessary. I'm fine. Really." She motioned behind her to where Danny, John, and the therapist, Dr. Burke, sat waiting.

John had a sour look on his face. He stood up and led Rose back to her lounge. "Dr. Burke wanted all of us here to show you our support."

Our support. Graham almost snorted with derision. What a difference half a year made. Not six months ago, John had threatened to take Rose to a mental health hospital, where he had fully intended on putting her through rounds of electroshock therapy and a lobotomy. The man was nothing short of a monster.

Graham led Helena over to the couch nearest his mother's, where Danny was sitting, and they took a seat beside his brother. Danny's pale blond hair had taken on a darker tint since he had started to recover, but it still carried a ghostly white cast that made his skin appear a bit green. Yet, as he smiled, Danny's eyes brightened.

"What's the craic?" Danny asked.

"Same thing, different day," Graham said. "How's it been going in the den of despair?" he whispered, motioning to the puckered faces around them.

Danny laughed, the sound light and airy, a sharp contrast to the dark and sucking air of the emotion-laden study.

"Come on now, you know there's nothing I like better than doctors and pity," Danny said with another eruption of cynical laughter. "Heya, Helena," he said, leaning around Graham so he could see her. "You're looking mighty fine today. Graham must be working you over well."

Helena's face turned a violent shade of red and her

mouth opened like she was going to speak, but nothing came out.

Dr. Burke stood up and opened up his little notebook like he needed a reminder of exactly whom he was there to treat and why. "Thank you all for coming to this meeting. I know I'm busy, and I'm sure that you are all as well."

Between the man's self-important tone and his posturing, Graham wanted to stand up and walk away. Thank Jaysus he only had to come here once to see the only man who specialized in paranormal issues. How his mother and Danny managed to put up with the over-inflated penguin on a weekly basis was beyond him.

"I thought it immensely important that we address the outstanding issues which are still present and active in and amongst your family dynamics."

Just when Graham thought things couldn't get any worse. Did the man understand the Pandora's box he wished to open? No. If he did, there was no way he would want to pursue this line of conversation—Graham's family had the market on domestic issues cornered.

John cleared his throat. "As a passive observer over the last few months, I wanted to thank you for the progress you've made with Rose and her mental health." He motioned toward his wife. "Just by looking at her, you can see the progress you have managed to make. She is so well put together. Job well done, Dr. Burke."

Arse kisser.

He must have been going for the Gold Star Award, or maybe the Husband of the Year Award. Either way, the therapist wasn't stupid enough to fall for John's act.

"While I appreciate your support, Mr. Shane, you are part of the reason we are where we are today."

Graham snorted with amusement.

John reached up and readjusted his expensive-looking silk tie. "I don't know what my *wife*"—Graham could almost see the acid drip off of John's tongue as he said the word—"has told you, but regardless of my complicity in her condition, I'm also the reason she is alive today. Without my financial backing and active contribution to her health care, it is my personal belief that she would have died long ago."

"So you're saying that she owes you her life?" Danny said, his voice low from lack of use.

John looked over at his son. "Danny, you and I both know the events that brought us here. Do you think you would be doing as well as you are today without me?"

Danny laughed, but it had lost its soft and playful sound. Instead it was hard, bordering on dangerous. "The only reason I'm here is because of Helena."

"I am bankrolling this estate. Without me—" John started to say.

Rose stood up and interrupted him. "Shut up. All of you shut up!"

A look of repugnance flickered over John's face.

"I told you this was a bad idea, Dr. Burke," she said, patting down the edges of her skirt. As she turned her wrist, the sleeve of her suit jacket raised, exposing a white bandage beneath.

"What in the hell is that?" John asked, jabbing his fat finger in the direction of her bandage. "What in the hell did you do?"

She pushed her sleeve down and glanced nervously over at the therapist.

"Let's not all jump to conclusions here," Dr. Burke said, thrusting both hands into the air like he was grasping for control of the situation.

"I thought you were stopping her from doing this... From making her act like she was going out of her mind," John said, his voice a wicked growl. "Don't you understand what I have risked to make sure my family was healthy?"

Dr. Burke's mouth opened and closed.

"You are fired," John said. "You need to leave and never come back. You're a fraud."

"I'm not a fraud, sir," Dr. Burke finally said. "If anyone in this room is a fake, it's you." He turned on his heel and fled the room, slamming the door in his wake.

John kept talking, almost manically, as he strode after the therapist. "He doesn't understand. No one understands," he repeated over and over under his breath.

"You all need to go," Rose said, walking to John and taking hold of him by the shoulders. "I've got him."

"What about you? Are you okay?" Graham gestured to his wrists.

"Don't worry. I wasn't trying to kill myself. I just had to tell him something. Everything got out of control, and he made assumptions. I'm fine; you don't need to worry about me."

"Does this have something to do with the *Codex*?" Graham asked, remembering the book that had once been hidden within the manor's walls—the book that had sent his brother and mother over the edge only a few years ago. "Please tell me you weren't using the book again."

His mother ignored him and his question, and quietly cooed sweet nothings to John, who was still repeating, "They don't understand…"

For a moment, it appeared as if the sickest person in the room wasn't the boy who'd spent years in a catatonic state or the woman they had assumed had tried to end her own life. Instead, it seemed to be the sweating, power-hungry man who paced the study like a rabid animal.

CHAPTER SIX

Just when Helena thought life couldn't get any more complicated, they had a murder on their hands, Graham's mother was possibly suicidal and refusing help, and Mr. Shane seemed to be going off the deep end.

Good or bad, they needed Mr. Shane to come back to himself and to his role as the leader of the manor staff. She and Graham had enough on their hands with the hospital, and the last thing they needed was to have to run the business of the manor in addition to the murder investigation. For now, they needed life to be as normal as possible—even if that meant suffering through the tumultuous nature of Mr. Shane's moods.

Maybe someday she would understand the man. On the other hand, maybe she didn't want to understand exactly what made him tick—or what had made him freak out.

Graham hung up his mobile and sat it on the table between them. The drawing room was full of tourists, and she couldn't help but wonder how many of them were here for the hospital's grand opening tomorrow. They had carefully selected guests from the families of those in their care, those whose relatives were supportive and involved in caring for their loved ones.

She couldn't wait for the celebration—finally there would be something positive in their lives, and maybe some of the seemingly perpetual stress would come to an end.

"The hospital staff has been talking." Graham motioned to his phone.

"And? Did anyone see anything that would give us any clues about Neill's death?"

He shook his head.

"Ya made it clear that Neill's death isn't to be talked about tomorrow, aye?"

"No one there is foolish. They don't want to lose their jobs or put anything at risk. I think they're going to stay quiet. At least for the event. As for after it's over, though…" He shrugged.

"What do ya mean?"

"They're scared. They don't know what's going on. And, just like us, they don't understand the death. At least they don't know it was a murder. Yet." He picked up his fork and pressed it into the bits of chicken he had pushed around on his plate while he'd been talking. "If…wait…*when* they find out. Well, you remember what happened last time; we ended up losing a quarter of our staff after Herb's death. We are going to have to work double time in order to stay open and keep the remaining staff happy."

He took a bite, chewing slowly, as if he wanted to savor this fleeting moment of peace.

He was right. If the staff found out more about Neill's

death, they would panic. Gossip would follow. Then the mob mentality would kick in. She and Graham would have to be careful how they navigated these waters.

"Do ya think this *event* is really even worth the risk of an investigation?" She couldn't believe she was uttering the words that Mr. Shane had said only a day before.

He gazed at her for a moment, but thankfully it was with a look of understanding, and it seemed he was carefully choosing his words. "The thought has crossed my mind. We *could* just let this go." He popped another bite into his mouth.

She waited for him to swallow as she thought over the ramifications a decision like this would have on their lives.

"If we don't go looking into this, maybe things will be okay. Maybe his death will just be swept under the rug. Things can just move along fine. No one would be any the wiser. There are only a few who know the truth," she said, trying to convince herself it was the right decision.

But deep in her gut, it just felt wrong. Something like this, the death of an innocent man, needed to be understood and atoned for. They needed to find out who had been behind it. If she and Graham didn't act now, what would happen if the person responsible murdered someone else? They would bear the blame, if only because they had failed to act.

Then again, if they actively pursued the case, everything—their relationship, Mr. Shane, Rose, her family, the hospital and its staff—could turn to dust beneath their fingertips.

"I don't know, Helena. I don't know what to do," Graham said, in a voice that was soft and pleading.

"Neither do I, Graham, but we can't just walk away."

Giorgio was busy handling the man's remains and looking into the hospital staff, and there was little they could do until he got back to them. They needed to act, but right now they were at an impasse. It would have been easy to walk away, but hard to look in the mirror.

Right now what she really needed was escape. She glanced back up at Graham, her eyes lingering on his stubble-ridden jaw. Her heart melted as she looked into his chocolate-colored eyes. They were deep and rich, warm in a way that swept into her core and made her think of the fantasy she'd had earlier. She squirmed in her chair.

What would it be like to have him in her bed? Would she be a sinner if she gave in to her need to be touched by a man?

She would be going against her culture and her traditions if she gave herself to a man before marriage. Yet, every part of her yearned to be touched by him. She needed to feel him against her skin. To feel his lips explore the curves of her body.

Her body shook, forcing her to move in her chair.

"Are you okay?" he asked, still looking at her with those stunning eyes.

"Aye, I'm fine."

"Really?"

How could she tell him that she needed a break from the stresses of life? More, that she wanted him?

"Do ya wanna get out of here?" she asked, motioning to the busy drawing room, where couples filled the tables around them.

He frowned. "What do you mean?"

She gave him a wicked smile. "I mean *do ya want to get out of here?*"

He cocked his head to one side like a confused pup before an impish smile flickered over his lips, accentuating the cleft in his chin. "Are you serious?"

She stood up and held out her hand for him to take hold. It felt so good to be in control of some element of her life for once.

He put his hand into hers. It felt strange, this role reversal, but it was empowering. Why did she have to wait for the man to make the first move? She could be a lady and still get exactly what she wanted from a man—even if it was sex.

It was as if a whole new door had opened in her soul as she realized the power she held. She could be the woman she wanted to be—at least in the bedroom. She didn't have to be held back by the restrictions her culture had placed on her. Or rather, she didn't wish to be. The stigmas and limitations of her past had held so much power over her, but why did she have to continue to let them? She had the right to make her own choices.

She'd already broken tradition by coming to live at the manor. Now it was time to continue following her heart.

Hopefully, she wouldn't regret it in the morning.

Then again, looking into Graham's hungry, needy eyes, she wondered if she was crazy to doubt herself. With a man as special as him, this couldn't possibly be a bad choice. He wasn't a one-night stand, or a man who meant nothing. They were going through a hard time. They needed each other. Now more than ever.

He stood up and followed her out of the room. She

couldn't help the way her hips seemed to sway as if they had a mind of their own. She felt sexier than she had in her entire life. Almost as if a whole new part of her soul had been awakened.

She was raw power.

"Do ya wanna go to your room?" she whispered, looking back over her shoulder at him as they left the hall.

"Uh." He paused, as though struggling to follow her train of thought. "I...Are you sure you want to go up there?" He looked at her with a mix of shock and awe, like he couldn't believe his luck, or understand what he'd done to earn this.

She was ready. Everything else in her life had pushed her into independence and womanhood—it seemed only right that her body should follow.

"It's been a long few months. We need this. *I* need to be close to someone. I need to be close to you."

His hesitation disappeared, and he wrapped his arms around her. "I...I can't believe—" He shut up, like he realized that he was possibly jinxing her offer. "If you're sure."

She loved the feeling of being in his arms. For the first time in a long time, she was safe. Like his touch promised her a reprieve from the reality that seemed to press in from all sides.

The closer they came to his room, the faster her heart beat, and she was sure if she wasn't careful, it would burst from her chest.

Apprehension nibbled at her, but she forced down the feeling. It was nothing more than social conditioning. What she was doing wasn't wrong. It was right, in so many ways.

Graham opened his door.

It had been a long time since she had been in this room. It smelled of his aftershave, a mixture of sandalwood and something reminiscent of green grass and the outdoors—it was the scent of a real man, and just the thought made her body clench with longing.

On the bookshelf was a collection of action books—John Grisham, Lee Child, and David Baldacci—but beside them were the works of Robert Frost and Walt Whitman. There was something so sexy about a man who loved to read about murder and mayhem and then, in the quiet hours, took time to skim through the weight of beautiful words—words that captured the soul and made a person question every aspect of their nature.

Across from his bed was a fireplace, a remnant of bygone days in which life had been slower, maybe even easier than the world she lived in now. Her thoughts drifted to when she and her siblings had been young and moving around the countryside. That was one of the things she missed the most about a life disconnected—gone were the moments by the fire, the quiet solitude of a morning in their campsite. Her life had changed so quickly.

And yet, here she was, ready for the next step. For a choice that might forever change her and her opinion of herself.

She let go of Graham's hand and made her way into the room. The bed was so close.

They had snogged, but never in a bed. Never even in his room. Being there now amplified every need she was feeling. She felt so…so naughty.

"If you want, we can just watch telly or something,"

Graham said, motioning toward the screen on the opposite wall.

It was nice of him to try and make her feel at ease, but that wasn't what she wanted. She wanted him to take her face in his hands, kiss her like it was the last time anyone on the planet would ever have the chance to kiss, and then show her how to get what she so badly wanted.

Then again, she couldn't judge him for acting like a gentleman. So many women would kill for a man like him—a man who had happily gone along with a relationship in which, for the last few months, he had been treated like a friend and given no promises of anything more.

For a second she wondered if she was making this decision partly because of her guilt and insecurity about her role in their relationship, but she pushed the thought aside. Guilt had nothing to do with the desire roaring through her.

She just had to stop overthinking, but the only way she could was by doing something she had no idea how to initiate.

What if she walked over to him, put her arms around him, and just took his lips in hers? Would things naturally progress? Was she just supposed to take off her clothes and get into bed? She'd seen enough telly to know there was a certain dance that always took place in moments like this, but suddenly she felt like she had two giant left feet.

Unsure, she walked across the room and stood in front of the fireplace. Three logs were stacked in the grate, waiting for the flame to be lit. They were so naked, so exposed, so vulnerable.

Vulnerable. The word reverberated through her. Was

she really ready to have him see all of her? To have him judge her for all of her flaws? To be open to and possessed by a man?

Graham stepped behind her and drew his arms around her waist. He bent down, his hot breath on her neck, and his lips slowly grazed the soft skin where her neck and her shoulders blended into one.

She sucked in a long breath as his tongue flicked against her skin.

"You are so beautiful," he whispered, his hot breath moving over her and making goose bumps rise on her arms and down her legs. "I've never wanted anyone or anything as badly as I want you. Right now. Right here. Are you sure you are ready for this?"

She wasn't sure of anything except how badly she wanted him. If she gave him this moment, if they shared it, maybe everything would fall back into place and their relationship could get back on track. She could prove her feelings to him and show him that no matter how hard things were, she still cared about him.

Helena nodded and turned her face, rubbing her cheek over his stubble. It made the nerves in her skin spark, and she yearned for his soft touch after the roughness. She turned her body in his hands, coming face-to-face with him. Even without a fire, she could feel the heat rising around them.

"I've wanted ya and this for as long as I've known ya." She moved close, so her lips were nearly touching his. "I'm sorry it's taken so long. I just…"

He leaned back and away from her lips. "You can't possibly be apologizing because you wanted to take your time.

You're allowed to take as much time as you need. I want you to be happy with this, and me. I don't want to force you into anything."

Any residual reservations she held dissipated into nothingness. He was sexy, but more than that, he was kind. That was a far bigger turn-on than the smooth contours of his chest or the muscles that pressed against the sleeves of his shirt. Superficial beauty was fleeting, but a beautiful soul was something that couldn't be replicated.

Leaning forward ever so boldly, she took his mouth with hers.

This was their moment.

His tongue skimmed over hers, and she lived in the pleasure of feeling his mouth exploring hers, diving deeper, making her hungry for more. Without breaking their kiss, she ran her hands down his shirt and pulled open his buttons as she moved closer to the bed.

He moaned into her mouth as she slipped the white shirt off his shoulders and let it drop to the floor. His kilt was next, and her mind wandered to the vision she'd had months ago. Was this the moment she had seen thanks to the forshaw? Was her fantasy going to become reality?

The dampness grew between her thighs at the thought of him teasing her with his nakedness, or maybe it was the way his lips moved down over her chin. His tongue flicked against her skin as he pulled open the first button of her shirt and exposed the tops of her warm breasts to the cool bedroom air.

His fingers trembled as he undid the rest of the buttons of her shirt. Was he really nervous? Or was it merely excitement that made his hands shake?

Maybe he was just as nervous as she was.

The thought was endearing.

Here he was, a man she assumed had been in a situation like this before, acting just as innocent as she did.

For a moment, she thought about bringing up the subject of how many women he had slept with, but decided better of it. Some things didn't need to be known. All she had to know was that he wanted her.

He pulled her shirt off, letting it drop to the floor upon his. He unclasped her bra, and the straps slipped down her arms and she dropped it at her feet. She covered her nakedness self-consciously. No one had ever seen her like this... this exposed.

"No," he said, shaking his head. "You don't need to cover yourself when you are with me. I want you to feel proud of who and what you are, always. You're beautiful." He reached up and gently pulled her hands down, away from her naked breasts.

The cool air caressed her nipples, making them grow hard.

He looked up at her as he took one nub into his mouth and swirled his tongue around it. She threw her head back with a wild moan at the feeling of his tongue on her flooded her senses.

This...him...it was all so fecking hot.

Her thighs trembled, and he pushed her down gently upon the bed. He stood between her open legs. Her skirt was hiked up, mere inches from revealing the rest of her.

For a moment he stood still, admiring her. "I'm the luckiest man alive," he said, half under his breath.

He reached down and unfastened the belt that held

his sporran in place. As she watched him, she slipped under the covers of the bed, pulling the white sheet around her middle.

"No," she said, watching him undo his kilt and let it slip down his thighs. "I'm the lucky one."

He held his red kilt with his left hand, so it just covered him. He smiled, the action impish and a bit shy, as though he were just as self-conscious.

She let the sheet drop from her hands as she reached out to him. "Come here."

He dropped the kilt, exposing all of him.

He was even better than she remembered from her vision. He climbed across the bed and slipped beneath the sheets beside her. Pulling her body against his, he reached down and ran his fingers over the edge of her skirt.

"It hardly seems fair that I'm the only one naked," he said with a wicked smile as he ducked beneath the sheets.

She drew in a breath as she lay back, resting her head on the pillow as his lips caressed the sensitive skin of her thigh. He trailed his tongue up her, to the edge of her skirt. When he reached her waist, he slowly, tooth by tooth, lowered the zipper. He pulled the skirt down her legs, kissing each spot where the fabric pulled against her skin.

The pleasure was agony, feeling him work over her skin, sucking and licking her as he moved to her panties.

She peeked under the sheet and watched as he lowered them down to her knees, slipped them over her toes, and let them fall to the mattress beside her skirt. He kissed up her leg, following an invisible trail that led, millimeter by millimeter, to her center.

His tongue hit her mark, and her body shuddered with

the ecstasy of the wonderful, powerful unknown. Her body went numb in all but the place their bodies had melded into one; there she could feel every stroke, every swirl of his tongue and vibration of his breath. It was so intense.

Almost too intense.

The world spun around her. The draw of the other world threatened to pull her away from the moment she had waited so long for.

This couldn't be happening. Not a vision.

No. Not now.

She'd waited so long to feel this with him.

Gray clouds swirled in her vision. She tried to focus on Graham, on his mouth, on the way his tongue slid over her, but his touch began to fade as her vision took hold.

A whine escaped her lips as she found herself standing naked in a swirling mass of gray clouds. Why had the Fates played this trick on her? Why couldn't she just have one moment to revel in her womanhood? One moment to escape the world? Or was that what this was? Was her subconscious playing tricks on her? Had her body become overwhelmed by the need to escape, so much so that she had accidentally triggered a vision?

The clouds started to pull apart, clearing away to reveal a darkened room. Old hospital beds and extra medical equipment filled the space. It was the old infirmary, the one tucked away in the bowels of the manor.

The place stank of fetid sickness and damp. She'd always hated the infirmary, but never more than now, standing there at the center of its ruins as the shadows of her vision pulled at her and called her into the infirmary's depths. She resisted, since somewhere deep within she felt that if she gave in, she would never return.

From somewhere in the darkness, she could make out the sound of a woman's faint cry. For a moment she thought about not following, about sticking to the place the vision had brought her, but her feet moved as though she were a puppet on a string. Her movements were jerky until she gave in, following the lead of whatever was pulling at her center.

Standing at the back of the infirmary, where the two wards came together, was Rose. She was wearing the same Chanel suit she'd been wearing at the meeting earlier in the day, but the edges were torn and plastered with dirt and blood.

"Rose?" Helena asked, forgetting for a moment that this wasn't reality or even the present.

Rose looked up. She glanced in Helena's direction, as though she had heard her voice through the waves of space and time. Though Rose was facing Helena, her eyes jumped from one position to another, glazed with a madness that only came to those of their kind.

What was happening? What had happened to Rose? Why was she here, tucked away once again in the place to which she'd said she never wished to return?

"I know you're here. I can feel you," Rose said, her voice hoarse and low, nothing like the light, airy tones the woman normally used.

There was something very wrong.

Helena wanted to run. To leave this place. To escape before it was too late.

Yet the harder she willed herself to end the vision,

the more the shadows at the edges of her sight seemed to become real, and pull her deeper.

No. No. This wasn't how it worked.

"I know you are here, Helena," Rose repeated. "You can't stop me. You can't stop this. Some things are greater than us. Some things are fated. We must listen to the gods. We must do as they order."

"No! Stop!" Helena said, as her body was jerked forward by whatever pulled the strings that controlled her. "I don't want this! Stop!"

Rose turned back to what had formerly been the nurses' station. Sitting open upon the counter was a large book. She started to chant words Helena didn't recognize. As she watched in panic, Mr. Shane formed from the ether of the shadows, materializing in front of her eyes.

Rose smiled as she looked upon her husband. "Have no worries, my dear, we're almost there. Together we will make things right. We will stop them. It's time."

CHAPTER SEVEN

He tried not to panic. Graham stroked her cheek gently. "Helena? Wake up. Please," he begged.

It had been six hours of no movement, just her steady breathing and open eyes, which stared into nothingness. With her eyes open, it made everything worse. It didn't seem as though she were asleep or just out of it—rather, she looked like she had crossed over the rainbow bridge.

He should never have let her come up to his room. He shouldn't have done what he'd done. This had to be his fault. Maybe it had all been too much stress. Maybe it had pushed her into this condition.

All the memories of Danny's early days in the catatonic state came flooding into his mind. What if that had happened to Helena? They both had the gift of seeing the future—it was more than possible they could suffer from the same affliction.

The guilt gnawed at him. Stress and emotional weight were Achilles' heels for their kind, for supernatural beings.

He knew this, yet he'd overlooked it all for a moment of pleasure—a stolen moment in which they could finally be together. As much as he wanted her, nothing was worth seeing her like this.

The nurse moved around the side of the bed. "Graham, if you want, you can leave her with us. We'll take right good care of her."

He had no doubt the nurse was speaking the truth—they loved her here—but he couldn't stand the thought of leaving her alone in the hospital. Not with Neill's death unsolved. For all he knew, they had an enemy within these walls.

And what if she woke up and he had gone? If that happened, he wouldn't blame her if she resented him, and he already feared what she would think when she awoke.

That was, *if* she awoke.

He tried to push the thought that she would be just like Danny from his mind—trapped in her body with nowhere to go, seeing only the darkest of human nature.

Danny had come back so different, so changed by his experience. The thought of Helena going through the same thing terrified him.

There was a soft knock on the open door, and he turned to see Danny and Rose waiting just outside.

"How's it going, my love?" his mother asked with a thin, comforting smile. "Have there been any changes?"

Graham shook his head as all the feelings he'd been trying to repress attempted to bubble to the surface. He just had to get through this. He couldn't concentrate on his feelings. He had to focus on getting Helena through this—any way he could.

Danny stepped beside them and slid his hand into Helena's without saying a word—and Graham loved him all the more for it. Right now, the last thing Graham wanted to do was talk. He wanted solutions—a fix for the agony he was going through—and if anyone could help, it was his brother.

Danny closed his eyes as he moved his thumb over the back of Helena's hand. He whispered something unintelligible as he stroked. Seconds turned into slow, painful minutes. It felt like an eternity as Graham stood watching.

Helena remained motionless, staring upward. She didn't move or respond.

Graham wanted to shake her, to pull her into his arms and make her wake up. Yet he knew there was no fixing her, not in the human way. No pulling her back to reality with a simple splash of water or archaic smelling salts.

"Can you see anything?" Graham asked, unable to control himself any longer.

Danny opened his eyes and stopped moving. "She's in deep."

"What does that mean? Where is she?"

Danny gave him a look—*the* look—that told him he probably didn't want to know, and Danny sure as hell wasn't going to tell him. His brother had spent so many hours in therapy and working with Ayre in the havari, and yet in all that time Danny had barely told him the ins and outs of what he'd experienced—only that he would never go back. That he would die if he were ever pulled back in.

Hopefully Helena wasn't thinking the same thing.

Could a person choose to end their life in a state like hers?

Another thought he couldn't handle. Not now.

"Aye," he said, nodding. "How can I help her?"

Danny put Helena's hand down on her belly, over the white blanket the nurses had pulled tight around her. "You can be here. Just like you were for me."

"Can you heal her?" Graham pressed, as he looked from Danny to his mother.

Rose bit her bottom lip. "Graham, son, you and I both know Danny isn't a healer. Don't put that pressure on him. He's gone through enough already."

Graham could almost hear the growls and see the snapping jaws of the caged wolf within him. She and John had been the cause of all this. If *they* hadn't brought them here, to this place, if they hadn't gotten greedy, if they hadn't used his brother, Helena wouldn't be here.

There were so many reasons to hate.

Danny reached over and put a hand on his shoulder, as if he could see the anger roiling within him. "She'll be okay. She's stronger than I am…than I ever was. She'll make it through this. You just need to—"

Keep his shite together.

"Aye," Graham said, not waiting for his brother to finish. "I know."

"I called your gypsy friend, Ayre—the one with the foreshaw," Danny said. "She's on her way. Maybe she can help."

"She can't heal."

"Nay," Danny said, his face falling. "But she holds a great deal of magic. I thought maybe she could do something."

They had to try something, anything that could make a difference in Helena's condition.

Ayre strode into the room. She smelled of herbs, perhaps lavender or mint; he couldn't quite make out the exact scent. It would have been soothing in any other venue, where IV pumps weren't beeping and nurses' voices didn't echo into the room from the hallway.

"'Ello, my dear. It's been a long time," she said, with a slight dip of her head in acknowledgment. "I'm sorry it has to be under these kinds of circumstances we keep seein' one another."

"Aye, but I'm glad you're here," he said.

"How'd this come about?" Ayre asked.

A faint heat rose in his cheeks as he thought of what had been happening and where they had been when Helena had fallen away. He could hardly admit it in front of his brother and mother.

"Would you mind excusing us for a moment?" he asked, moving to the door and motioning gently for his family to step outside.

They moved to the hall, and his mother gave him a questioning look as he closed the door behind her.

He didn't need any of her inquiries right now—at least, none that would pry into his private life. Helena had been hesitant enough to take things to the level they had; she would be mortified if she came to know he'd told the entire world about what they'd done.

"Am I to be thinkin' you're not proud of how she came to be like this?" Ayre asked, her tone serious and dry.

"It has nothing to do with my pride."

At least not in the sense in which she meant it.

"Then?"

"We were...*exploring* each other when she just...I don't know. It was like when she has a vision. I thought she'd come back. I waited. Then, when she didn't come back after thirty minutes, I got her dressed and I brought her here. I still don't know what's wrong with her."

"Exploring..." She rolled the word around on her tongue as if she were trying to find a spot where it would fit against her cheek. "Aye, I see."

She walked to the side of the bed, where Danny had been standing. Rather than touching Helena, she raised her hands over Helena's chest and took in a long breath. Her eyes rolled back into her head, and she exhaled.

Dropping her hands to Helena's chest, she stood silent and still.

A smile overtook her face, and she looked up at Graham.

"She's okay."

"How do you know?" he asked in a single breath, afraid that if he believed her, even for a moment, that everything would turn to dust.

"I caught a glimpse of her future. *Your* future," Ayre said, reaching up and pushing a hair from Helena's forehead. "She and you...you're a good match. The Fates have done well. But nothin's gonna be easy for the two of ya. You are always gonna have to work. Complacency will only bring resentment. But I'm thinkin' you already know this..."

Sometimes having someone around who had the gift of sight wasn't as great a thing as he would have imagined— they saw everything, even the things that everyone tried to hide.

Maybe he had grown complacent.

"Is that why this happened? I've been too inattentive?"

Ayre shook her head. "Ach, the fault doesn't rest on your shoulders alone. Stress can be hard on any relationship, especially a buddin' one." The beads in Ayre's hair fell over her shoulder, clicking together as she leaned forward and drew in a long breath. "What happened in this place?"

Graham frowned, not following her rapid change of thought. "What?"

"Someone died here." She took in another deep breath, scenting the air. "A man. Murder. What happened?"

"We don't know." And honestly, at the moment, he didn't care. All he cared about was Helena's well-being. "It's fine, though. Everything has been taken care of."

"Disposing of the body will hardly solve your problems with that man." Ayre looked up at the ceiling and started to walk toward the window at the far side of the room.

What did she know about it?

She turned to face him. What, did she have the ability to read minds as well?

"Okay," he said, afraid maybe she *could* read his mind, though he knew it was unlikely.

"Whoever was behind that man's death is gonna kill again. They wanna kill many. Their soul is black with hate. You need to be careful."

"Who's behind it?"

Ayre smiled. "My vision isn't perfect—you know I'm only given what the Fates and the gods wanna show me, and even then what I see ain't always exactly what comes to pass. I don't hold the answers you are lookin' for, no matter how badly you'd like me to."

"Who does the person want to kill?" Graham asked, trying to ignore the dull ache in his gut.

"I...I dunno. They're driven by rage. By some feeling of injustice."

"Did John kill him?"

"No, I don't get the sense that he did." Ayre shook her head. "I wish I could give you more...The shadows are holdin' more, but they won't let me in."

He nearly laughed as he thought about the position he was in—with one woman who couldn't reach far enough into the shadows, and another who couldn't escape them. The Fates were cruel.

Until that moment, he'd never really thought about the fact that the Fates must have enjoyed the pain they inflicted, the strings they pulled, and the madness they caused.

"They, the killers or the Fates or the gods or whoever, they don't want to hurt Helena, do they?" Graham asked, once again terrified by the future.

"She's in danger. I can feel it upon her. You need to pull her from the depths. She needs to leave this place." Ayre peered up at him. "You all need to leave this place. No one's safe. The veil...it's bringin' danger upon us all."

"What veil?"

"The veil that rests upon these grounds. It's always thin, but thanks to the alignment of the planets, it's even more thinly stretched than usual. As you know, there be great power here, and there are people who know that and want to tap into it. They'll stop at nothin' to get what they want and need. Even if it means killin'."

"Let me get this right. Someone wants to use the psychic power of this place? For what?"

"Ach, I dunno. But with a black soul, you can assume they ain't plannin' on makin' a positive change." Ayre shook her head. "I don't normally subscribe to the idea that there are two types of magic. Magic be magic. There is good; there is bad, and there are times where it can be both—it all depends on the perspective of the practitioner. Yet, in this case, I got no doubt that they want to burden the world with their black magic."

He thought of the *Codex Gigas*, still hidden within the manor. Did this person's hunger for power mean that they knew about the book? Was that part of the reason they had descended upon this place?

"Are there other places in the world like this, with a thin veil?"

"The closest is in England, and there are many places on this planet that are sacred and used to access the ethereal realm. You're not alone."

"Then why here? Why now?"

Ayre shrugged. "I'm not one who can claim to understand the workings of this world. Lotta things are a mystery to me. If I had all the answers, I would no longer be human—I would be a god."

His thoughts still on Neill, Graham took out his mobile and pulled up the picture he'd taken of the man's brand. "Have you ever seen this marking before?" He was grasping at straws, but it was the only clue he had to work with.

Ayre took the phone and stared at the image. "Huh. I can't say that I have." She scrolled to the next picture, one with Neill's face in full view. "Is this the dead man?"

He nodded. "Know him?"

"I wish I could say that I do, but nay, he's a stranger to me."

He hated this feeling of powerlessness. She had warned him Neill's killer would strike again, but he was to start his investigation with nothing to point him in the right direction.

"Have you asked them?" Ayre pointed toward Graham's family, peering in from the other side of the safety glass.

John stood with them now, looking in at Helena. The manic edge he had carried during their meeting with the therapist had disappeared, and his stoic nature seemed to have returned. And, as he noticed Graham looking, he gave him a firm nod.

A note of anger roiled up from Graham's depths at his stepfather's appearance. John had made it clear that he cared nothing for them—especially Helena. His presence was nothing more than a show for the hospital staff.

Graham sighed, letting the anger melt away. It wouldn't help for him to be angry right now. And going by John's display with the therapist, maybe now wasn't the time to put any more stress on the man. Regardless of how pompous and strong he seemed, or the show he put on, he was clearly dealing with something.

Graham looked to Ayre. "Have you been talking to John?"

"No. Why?"

He didn't want to tell her how he had seen his stepfather acting. It didn't matter—at least not to her. And maybe it was nothing more than a momentary break for the normally well-put-together businessman. Everyone had their moments.

Graham motioned for them to come inside. John followed behind his mother and Danny. He kept his gaze low, like he was embarrassed about his earlier display. It only made the weirdness Graham had been feeling toward him intensify. Something was definitely amiss.

"John, are you okay?" he asked, not bothering to dance around the issue.

"I'm fine," John said, jerking his gaze up from the floor in a forced display of dominance. "How's Helena?"

So he wanted to put on the show. Fine. Aye.

"She's doin' better," Ayre said, taking control of the conversation. "She's just a wee bit knackered. We just need to love and support her right now. And not be burdenin' her with our troubles." She looked between him and John as she spoke. "Graham has a picture he'd like you all to see. Don't you, Graham?"

He clicked the screen back on and flipped back to the image of the brand. "Do any of you recognize this marking?"

Rose and Danny took a quick look and shook their heads, but when John took the mobile, what little color left in his face drained away.

"What's the marking? What does it mean?" Graham pressed.

John clicked the screen off and handed the mobile back to him. "I have no idea. I've never seen that kind of thing before."

Just the thin sheen of sweat that was covering his forehead proved he was lying.

"Don't play me for a fool, John. You know what that is. Tell me."

John turned to Rose and slipped his hand into hers. "I don't know what the marking means. Besides, what does a dead man's brand have to do with Helena?"

Though it was possible John could have put the pieces together and figured out that the brand was Neill's, no one had told him—which meant he knew a hell of a lot more than he cared to show.

"Ayre, tell him what you told me, about the murderer."

"It's just a vision, Graham, but you all need to take action to find the people behind the murder. They're only beginnin'."

"They?" Danny asked.

Ayre nodded. "Only one person killed Neill, but there are others behind him. Others who want dark things. From what I was shown, their souls are as black as midnight, and they fear only their failure."

"Who?" Danny continued.

Graham gave Ayre's hand a reassuring squeeze. "She doesn't know. And I have nowhere to start. All I have is this," Graham said, lifting his mobile. He looked to John. "That's why it's vital you tell me anything you know."

"Ayre must be mistaken. You know how fickle the gift of sight can be. It may be showing her something that never happened, and may never happen. Neill's death has already been ruled a suicide by my man. This needn't go any further."

"You know his death wasn't a suicide. If you don't actually do something, many other lives could be in danger." Graham tried to keep the bitterness from his voice, but it was nearly impossible. "Do you really want more blood on your hands?"

CHAPTER EIGHT

The world was dark, and no matter how hard she tore at her reality, Helena couldn't break through the thick nothingness. It was like a black litter bag pulled tight around her body, and with every second that passed, she was one second closer to suffocation.

She couldn't let them win. She couldn't let her affliction stop her from experiencing the world. She couldn't fall into the depths and not return.

No.

She sobbed.

She couldn't.

There was a voice near the edge of her consciousness, barely audible through the thick plastic nothingness; the sound was familiar, soft, and airy. Helena strained to hear, feeling nearly deaf in the reverberating silence.

There it was again. The voice. She reached for it like a child starved of human contact.

It was a woman's voice. "She's going to be fine. Don't fight with your father."

"Stepfather." She recognized Graham's voice.

"You know what I mean," the woman said, her voice becoming loud enough that Helena could tell it was Rose.

Was she having another vision?

"He's done so much for this place. We've all made mistakes. And if he says the death was suicide, I'm sure it was a suicide."

"Mother, why are you sticking up for him?"

"Graham, love, I just trust that he has his reasons. He's not an evil man."

"No more fightin'," Helena whispered, trying to stop her mind from pulling her deeper into the blackness as their words forced her farther into the recesses. "Please...no..."

There was the touch of a hand on her cheek, and she reached up, but there was nothing there.

Her heart threatened to implode. Was this her new reality? Half-feeling and stuck in perpetual blackness, but able to hear the world moving forward without her? This feeling—it had to be what hell felt like. Or was it purgatory?

"Helena?" Graham's voice broke through her thoughts. "Come back to me, my love."

Did he really love her? He had told her that he loved her once, but it had been so long ago that the words seemed more like a fantasy. He had even spoken of marriage, but she had put him off.

It was no wonder he hadn't spoken of love again. Perhaps she had broken his heart. Once a thing like that was broken, the stitches of time and the glue of words could mend it, but it would never be quite the same again—and while the mind might forget the trauma, the heart never would.

"Helena?" Graham asked again.

Far away, at the edges of the blackness, a light rose from the darkness. A tunnel.

Was this it? Was this what the end of life looked like?

No. She had so much more to do. So much more to experience. She wasn't ready.

"Graham," she called, hoping he would somehow come to her rescue and pull her free of her fears.

"It's okay, my love," he whispered, his voice closer. "Fight. You are strong. You have to come back. I need you. *We* need you."

We? Who was he talking about?

The orb of light grew, enveloping her and making the chill that had filled her start to drift away.

There was the feeling of a touch on her cheek. She reached for it, and this time her fingers grazed over Graham's. His fingers were warm, and as she touched him, he stopped stroking her face and took hold of her hand.

"Are you there? Are you really there?" he asked, his tone slightly high and panicked, as though afraid he might be getting it wrong.

She forced her eyes open. Graham and his family were standing around her, even Mr. Shane, but no one from her family was there. Wherever *there* was. The bright fluorescent lights burned her eyes, forcing her to grimace.

"Where am I?" she asked, her voice hoarse and almost robotic even to her own ears.

"We brought you to the infirmary," Graham said.

She gasped as she remembered the infirmary in her

vision. Had they brought her to the bowels of the manor? Was Rose setting to work to…Helena tried to recall exactly what Rose had been doing, but she couldn't quite make heads or tails of what she'd seen. All she could think of was the feeling of danger and fear that had risen within her as she'd watched Graham's mother.

Her hand tightened on Graham's. "No. Get me out of here. I can't be here." She glared at Rose.

The woman had a confused look on her face. "What's the matter, dear?"

"Get out," Helena said, her voice quiet.

Rose didn't move.

She tried again, this time with more force. "Get. Out."

Graham looked over at his mother and motioned for her to step out. Mr. Shane took Rose by the hand and led her from the room.

Ayre stood at the end of the bed, smiling knowingly.

"When you're ready, child, I'm around. You come find me. We'll talk. For now, rest." She moved to walk out of the room with Danny, but stopped and turned back. "And don't worry about what hasn't yet come to pass. Our visions can be wrong, my child. You know this. We are only given the moment in time the Fates have chosen."

The woman was talking in riddles again, but now, thanks to the banging in her head, Helena couldn't handle the pain of trying to decipher the woman's words. Helena answered with a simple nod, but Ayre gave her that familiar knowing and disapproving look as she led Danny from the room. "I'm here for ya. Always," Ayre repeated as she closed the door behind them.

Graham glanced back at Helena with a look of deep concern on his face. "What happened? What did you see?"

Helena's hands were shaking, though she didn't know exactly why.

She wasn't sure if she wanted to tell him the truth or not. Maybe Ayre was right. Maybe the vision was wrong. But Helena couldn't shake the terror that filled her. Rose had meant to hurt someone, but whether it was Helena or someone else, she couldn't be sure.

A terrible thought struck her. What if Rose had been behind Neill's death?

She rolled the idea through her mind. Rose wasn't big enough to have taken Neill down—even hurt, Neill would have been stronger than the petite woman. There was no way she could have been responsible for his death, and that was to say nothing of the fact that he had been strung up from the roof. She couldn't have easily reached the ceiling, and it was doubtful she could have lifted the body.

Helena sucked in a long breath and tried to gain control over her frenzied thoughts.

Even her vision with Graham in his bedroom had been inaccurate. Nothing was set in stone, not when it came to the future. Maybe it had just been a way for the world to warn her of something, or set things on a different course. Or maybe it was just a vision sent to torture her and make her question her own sanity.

Her thoughts fluttered to her vision of Graham. His red kilt. Standing beside the bed as she waited for him to slide in beside her. She squirmed as she remembered exactly what had happened.

She looked up to Graham. "Are you okay? Ya know, after what happened in your room."

He opened his mouth to speak, but guppied for a moment. "Am I okay? You're the one in the hospital bed who just went a bit mad on my mother." He paused. "Are *you* okay?"

She looked down at her arms, where she'd been jabbed and prodded and IVs had been stuck into her veins. Reaching down, she pulled on the lines, ripping the clear tape from her skin and pulling out the needles that fed liquid into her body.

"I'm fine. I just need to get out o' here. I shouldn't be here. It was just a vision." She spoke fast, her words coming as quickly as her thoughts.

She had no idea what to do, where to go, or how to explain things to Graham, and shrouding it all was her embarrassment. They'd finally taken the next step in their relationship, and she and her *gift* had managed to ruin it all.

When would she be done failing?

As she stood up, a cold draft wafted over her skin, which was barely covered by the hospital gown. Graham looked away, giving her a moment to pull the back of the gown closed. He had just seen her naked in his bedroom, but now he didn't seem to want to look at her again. Was he feeling just as embarrassed as she was? Or had he been unimpressed with what he'd seen?

She tried not to consider the latter possibility. No man in history had ever looked at a naked woman and not really wanted to look at her again. No matter the woman's size, shape, or ethnicity—men were born to love the female form. Sure, there may have been some they liked better, but like her da used to say, "There's a lid for every pot." But what if she wasn't the lid that Graham was looking for?

For a moment, she considered closing the blinds and stripping down just to test his reaction. She would know immediately whether or not he thought her naked body was beautiful.

But then she thought back to the way his body had pressed against hers. He had responded to every touch, every kiss. Maybe she was just being overly sensitive.

She walked to the small closet at the corner of the room. Hanging inside was a fresh set of clothes Graham must have brought down for her.

"Where did ya put the clothes I had on?"

Graham walked over to the windows to the hall and pulled the blinds closed so she could have a bit of privacy.

"I had your sister bring you a set of clothes up from the cottage, and she took the others to be laundered."

Helena was a bit relieved. First, because her family had been to see her and Angel had come to help, and second, because Graham hadn't been the one to sift through her knickers and pullovers trying to find clothes.

"Why didn't she stay? Kids?" Helena yanked on the pullover and jeans and slipped her feet into her shoes. Her arm ached where she had freed herself from the IV. There would definitely be a bruise tomorrow.

"Actually, she said she had some errands to run, and apparently there's some big rally goin' on in Adare."

"What kind of rally?"

Graham shook his head. "I don't know, but she said it was making it hard to get around, and the locals are starting to complain."

"Does Mr. Shane know about it? He's gonna be upset if he thinks it's interferin' with the grand openin' tomorrow." She glanced at the windows leading to the hall. "Is he still here?" She grabbed her purse, which Graham had set on the floor of the closet.

Graham walked to the door and cracked it open. "No. I think he wanted to run Rose and Danny back to the manor." He clicked the door shut and checked his watch. "If you're feeling up to it, I have an idea."

"Huh? An idea about what?"

"About Neill. I was thinking about his employment records. Maybe we can find out where he's from, or why someone would have a grudge against him—it's probably pointless, but we got to start somewhere. If Ayre was right, we need to move fast."

"What if this is just some random killing? Ayre said the person has a black soul. Maybe they're killing for the thrill of it or somethin'." She motioned to the bed. "Everyone in this place has real issues, many of which are psychological. Just look at what happened to me. I had no idea where I was, or what I was doin'. What if I had been possessed? For all I know, I could have been out of my mind, killing randomly."

"I think we would've noticed if someone who was a danger to others was out of their room. Security is tighter than it was before. The nurses learned their lesson. And Giorgio has accounted for all the patients and staff, save a few who were on break."

"Not everyone in this place can have an alibi, Graham. If that were correct, then a murder would have never occurred. Whoever killed Neill had to have been in this building—"

"Or had access to the inner building."

"Or found a way to gain access from the front desk."

Graham gave a resigned sigh, like he was frustrated with the onslaught of questions and the lack of available answers. "There has to be something we're missing."

CHAPTER NINE

The sounds of horses neighing from their stalls echoed toward them as Graham and Helena made their way through the back entrance of Clonshire Equestrian Center. A black mare stuck her head out over her gate, gave them a curious glance, and smacked her lips as though to say that if they gave her a pellet, she would stay quiet.

Helena gave a light laugh. "At least we know someone we can pay off." She walked to the bucket that rested near the haystack, grabbed a handful of pellets, and generously offered them to the nosy mare.

"Where's the horse that fell on Neill? Is it okay?" Helena asked, motioning around the stalls.

He hadn't thought much about the piebald gelding. "He seemed to be fine." Graham walked down the row of stalls to the one marked with the horse's picture. Beneath the image was the name "Rough and Tumble."

Helena let out a small laugh. "Aye, they named him right."

The gelding poked his head over the door and drew in a long breath, huffing as he took in their scent. He whinnied in recognition and threw his head as he looked toward Graham.

"He remembers ya," Helena said.

Graham walked over to the horse and scratched his forehead, right under his mane. The horse tilted his head slightly, as if encouraging him to scratch just a bit harder. Graham looked over the horse's body. He seemed to be standing well, shifting his weight from foot to foot in a normal way, and there were no cuts or visible marks. If he hadn't known that this was the horse that had rolled over Neill, he wouldn't have suspected the animal had been involved in what should have been a deadly accident.

For a moment, he wondered if maybe this was another joke the Fates were playing. It was like they were showing him and Helena that no matter how hard they—or rather, Helena—tried to save a life, it was really the Fates who controlled a person's destiny. No mortal being, not even one with gifts, could alter the Fates' plans forever.

Or maybe there was no such thing as the Fates. Perhaps they were all merely moved around this plane of existence by simple forces of action and reaction, small choices that led either one way or the other. Maybe what happened in people's lives was nothing more than cosmic randomness. If not, he hated to think why the Fates had chosen to make life hard—or what mistake *he* had made to call this mess down upon them.

"I'm sorry about what happened." Helena stepped beside him and ran her hand down the other side of the gelding's face.

"Huh?" Graham asked, trying to follow her train of thought.

"I mean, back in your bedroom. I didn't mean for me to…ya know. I wish I could stop what's happenin' to me. I just…I'm sorry."

A thin layer of sweat rose on his skin. "Don't be sorry. You can't control everything. And you losing yourself to your vision wasn't your fault." It had been his. He had thrown her over the edge. He caused her to lose herself—and not in a good way. "It was mine. We shouldn't have…"

"We shouldn't have tried to make love?" she said, her voice barely above a whisper, but full of strength. "That's crazy, Graham. We need to have a relationship that's full. If I hadn't waited so long, maybe…"

"Stop. You should never feel rushed or pushed into doing anything you don't want to. We can keep waiting. We don't have to do anything again until you're ready."

Helena remained silent for a moment. "But what happens if I always react like that? What happens if it gets worse?"

"You might never have a reaction like that again. We don't know, but we can't let the fear of what could happen stop us from living." As soon as he'd spoken he wished he could take the words back. "But I never want to hurt you. I don't want you to—"

"End up like Danny did?" she said, finishing his thought.

He traced his hand down the gelding's face until he gently brushed the tips of Helena's fingers. "I never want you to be unhappy, or to put you at risk. I care about you too much."

She wrapped her fingers around his and lifted them to her lips and gave the backs of them a soft kiss. "I care about ya too. That's why I think maybe it's best if I just get out of the way of ya livin' your life."

"What?" Was she really breaking up with him because they both feared sex? "No. That would be giving up. We'll find a way to get around this. We can try to make love again. We'll move slow, talk to each other. If you think you're feeling anything that you shouldn't be, then we can stop. We'll learn each other's bodies."

"What if that never works, Graham? I don't want ya to have a life half-lived. I want ya to be able to make love, to not fear hurting the person you're with because ya want to express yourself in a physical way. If something happens, I don't think I'd be the one who'd pay the highest price—I think it would be you. Ya were already wracked by guilt after what happened. Can ya imagine if I spent a year like that? A lifetime? One simple thing. One choice that we should be able to make would ruin your life. You'd never let yourself fall into the arms of a lover again—you'd be stripped of that pleasure."

"We can't be afraid of what could happen, Helena. We just have to face the world as we know it and move forward one step at a time."

"You're right, Graham, but we can't stick our heads in the sand and pretend like what we fear ain't a possibility. Maybe it's best for both of us if we just take a step back. You can date whomever you like. Someone more like you. Someone who ya don't have to fear touchin'." She pulled her fingers from his. "Someone who doesn't fear you touching them."

"You fear me?" His heart sank to a depth he hadn't been aware it was capable of reaching. It was like the organ had fallen out of his chest and been kicked across the floor.

This wasn't his first relationship, but it was the most real, the most emotionally fulfilling of his life—and she *feared* his touch. What was more, he couldn't blame her. He feared it equally.

He took a step back. "This isn't what I want. I don't want to lose you over something so…unimportant."

She moved to reach for him but dropped her hand. "You've been so patient. So kind with me. You've waited for me. You've done everything right. Yet what happened today, it just proves that maybe we are tryin' to make somethin' work that we shouldn't be. We can't…we can't be together, Graham."

He heard only the sounds of horses and the echoing ring of her pain-inducing words. This couldn't be over. He loved her too much to let her go over something fixable, or at least survivable. He couldn't let her push him away in some ill-conceived attempt to protect them both. He didn't need protection, not when it came to giving her his heart.

"Not every first time is perfect. Sex and life are imperfect, and they can be beautiful in their imperfections. If we can just try again…" Even he could hear the pleading in his voice.

He never thought he would be the type who would beg to keep a woman, but he definitely wasn't the kind who would walk away from something as good as what they had. Sure, things hadn't been flawless. Sure, they had grown a bit complacent in their relationship, and the stresses of life had come between them. They had cultural differences, but when push came to shove, they really weren't that different. They were just two people who wanted to share their hearts, to share their lives with one another—that was, until now.

He felt like he'd been defeated by the world, and the only person he wanted to turn to was Helena.

The door that led from the arena to the horse stalls opened. A man stood just outside the doorway. His shoulders were stooped with age, and his bald spot caught the thin light of the barn. He had his back turned to them and was talking loudly with someone Graham couldn't see.

"That boy was a fecking eejit. I told him to have nothing to do with those people. He was only supposed to be a silent observer. If he hadn't made a mistake, he'd still be alive. He knew the risks he was taking."

Graham slid open the bolt to the gelding's stall, pushed Helena in, and followed her before quietly closing the gate and sliding the bolt back into place. They couldn't be caught breaking into the equestrian center. The horse huffed and moved around as he tried to make sense of their presence in his area.

"Whoa, baby," Helena whispered, trying to calm the nervous animal.

The gelding calmed, but threw his head in protest.

Helena pushed deeper into the shadows and motioned for Graham to follow, but he waved her off.

"Murdering Neill was reckless," the other man said, answering the balding man from the shadows.

"No, *he* was reckless. We were proactive."

"I'm sure he thought he was being proactive as well."

"Neill was a maggot. We can both agree on that, but he's no longer a problem. Now we just need to find a way to keep moving forward with our plan," the balding man said. There was the sound of his shoes scraping through the bits of hay and dirt that littered the floor.

"Is everything in place?"

Graham tried to look through the bars to see the men who were talking about Neill's death, but he couldn't see them without completely exposing himself. These were men who weren't afraid to murder, to reach their goals by any means necessary, and Graham doubted they would blink at the thought of killing him and Helena for eavesdropping.

"With everything that happened today, there's been a lot of traffic around the area. We had a harder time getting in. I'm sure everything will be put in place, but it's going to take a little more time," the balding man said.

"And yet you are wasting your time looking after a bloody horse," the other man grumbled. "It's alive, aye?"

"Do you know how much this horse cost? How much money it could make us? It has a bloodline better than yours."

"It's still a horse. It's like you care more about it than you did for our man. Our man could have done quite a bit more for our fight. Do I need to remind you that there is a whole building full of freaks at our fingertips? They are the ones we need to worry about. They are going to contaminate us all with their vile ailments."

The man stopped just short of the gate, and Graham pushed back into the shadows, standing in front of Helena and keeping her from view. Regardless of their relationship status, he was always going to protect her.

The gelding moved toward the front of the stall and stuck his head out, just like he had done when Graham and

Helena had made their way into the barn. The horse whinnied, the sound almost like a show of strength. Graham liked the thought that perhaps even the horse was trying to protect them.

"Look, the filthy beast is fine."

"He's not a filthy beast. He did nothing wrong."

"No, he only tried to kill a man and nearly got us all found out. What would have happened if the gypo had touched Neill and read his mind?"

"That's not what she can do. Apparently all she can do is heal, and she has a minor ability to see the future."

"Minor ability?"

"From what I've heard from the staff, her visions are sporadic, like today. She can't control them. They don't always come true. More of a liability than an asset if you ask me."

"None of their gifts are assets. They're abhorrent, and the people like her—they're freaks. All of them."

Helena moved, like she was going to push around him and face the men who were spewing hate, but he stopped her. This wasn't the time for her to go running out. She wouldn't change the men's minds by going toe-to-toe with them. These men were dangerous. They wouldn't hesitate to hurt someone in their way—especially a gypsy who had broken into the center. But Graham would never let them lay a finger on the woman he loved.

"Stay here. Don't let them see you," he said in the quietest whisper he could. He stepped forward and out of the shadows. "Stay safe."

He pressed his body against the rough wood of the stall's wall and made his way to the door. Peeking out, he could just discern the back of the man's gray suit and his balding head. From this angle the man looked like an over-fattened snake, round in the middle, with a neck that blended into his corpulent body.

"Let's go," the other man ordered.

"Aye, fine." The obese man stepped away from the stall.

Hopefully the man's lethargy was mirrored by the man in the shadows, but Graham couldn't believe that they would be that lucky. They had just witnessed something that told him all he needed to know—Ayre had been right. Neill was only a small part of something so much larger—something where blackness reigned.

CHAPTER TEN

Staring up at the ceiling as she lay on the lumpy, decades-old couch that sat in the center of the cottage, Helena couldn't decide what she hated worse—herself, or the feelings that still threatened to overpower her. She was so confused and full of regret.

It had been a mistake to break up with Graham. He hadn't done anything wrong. He was a good man, and they complemented each other in so many ways. In fact, she had spent more than her fair share of time imagining their future: the children they would have, where they would live—even that they would always keep a bottle of Jameson in the house for guests.

Maybe a drink was exactly what she needed now. It would fix the way she was feeling—or at least numb it enough that she was able to forget. Then again, if she took that path, she would be that much closer to repeating the mistakes her mam had made and perpetuating the cycle she hated so much.

She would just have to find something else to help her cope. Over the last few months, any time she had a problem, she could turn to Graham.

How could she have missed the ways she had come to depend on him and their relationship?

She had been stupid to only look at the little problems—the moments missed because they had been busy, those times they couldn't give each other exactly what the other needed. It was called life. But she had thought that it would be ideal—that they would never have moments of anything less than bliss.

Maybe it was just the fact that this was the first time a relationship had moved past the honeymoon phase. Hell, it had been the only real relationship she'd ever had. Maybe she had just fallen into the traps set by their cultural differences. They were bound to not always understand one another, but if they had talked more and learned more, they could have found a way. They had just lost so much time fighting the world around them, a world that hated their supernatural abilities and told them what they could and couldn't be, that maybe for a moment she had let the world win.

She got up from the couch, made her way to the kitchen, and started the tea water. There were the sounds of footsteps coming down the hall and turned to see her da.

There were dark circles under his eyes, like he hadn't slept. And, as she looked at him, she couldn't help but notice that in the last few months, he had come to look even older than the day he had stepped out of the clink.

"Gra, it's early. Why are ye up? Ye should be asleep," Da said, glancing over at the clock on the back of the stove.

"I could ask ya the same question, Da."

He answered with a tired smile. "It's been a long week, and I've still not got everything done I need to be doin'. I never thought workin' at the manor would be this hard."

She understood his sentiment completely. "I never thought life would bring us to this place, that's for sure."

"Aye," he said, taking out two cups for tea and setting them on the counter. "This's a strange world that we live in. Ain't it?" He bent down to grab something from the bottom cupboard. As he moved, his shirt rose slightly, and Helena could make out long red cuts across his back.

"Da, what happened to ya?"

He immediately stood up and pulled his shirt low, covering the marks. "Nothin', gra. I'm fine."

"No. What happened to your back?"

"Really, gra. It's nothin'. I just had a bit of an accident when I was workin' on one of the cottages."

As he moved, she noticed he seemed to put more weight on his left foot.

"Did ya fall?"

She wanted to lift his shirt and get a better look at the marks, but she knew he'd never let her. He wasn't the kind of man who wanted a woman to worry about him. He was the head of the family, the strong one, the one who carried the burden and refused to share it with others. He was and would always be a Traveller, and their culture didn't allow them the more fluid gender roles that were part of the lifestyle of country folk. That fluidity was something she had grown to love over her months in the manor, but no matter how much she wished it were a part of her culture, the times wouldn't change rapidly enough for it to become a part of her life—at least, if she ended up with a Traveller.

She sighed. The only man she really wanted to end up with was Graham. She was addicted. And she had a feeling that no matter what state their relationship was in, she would always be thinking of him. No amount of time would break the spell he had cast on her heart—especially if she continued working at the hospital, in such close proximity to him.

Maybe she and the fam should leave. They could all get back on the road.

Graham would be safer if she left. He wouldn't have to worry about their relationship, or lack thereof. She wouldn't continue to put him at risk by staying there. And Angel and the boys, they could get back in touch with their Traveller roots.

Being settled, the boys would never know the enchantment that could be found in constant, beautiful movement. Every day it was something new: a different place, a different neighbor, and sometimes they even came across new ways of thinking. They would listen to the stories of their people, the folklore and the *sean nós* sung beside the campfire each night.

And Da…Helena looked at him as he poured the hot water over the tea and swirled the bag lazily, waiting for it to steep.

"Da, do ya like being here?"

He turned slowly, as though his body hurt. "I like it here just fine, gra. Why?"

His face remained placid, unmoved by any emotion

as he spoke, which only made her wonder what exactly he was thinking.

"I mean, do ya miss it? The traveling? The campsites?" She motioned to the walls that surrounded them.

He looked at the wall and gave a resigned sigh. He handed her the tea, as though he were using it to take a moment to collect his thoughts.

"Truth be told, gra, I do. I miss it. And I miss my Cora."

Her mouth dropped open. How could he miss her mam, the woman who had done nothing but fight with him? The woman who had taken his daughter and run away? The woman who had risked their children's lives?

"What?" she asked in a breathless whisper.

"Before I went to prison, when you were small, things between her and me, well, we got on just fine. She was good in those days. Loved horses. Loved to make everyone happy. It was the first time I found myself in trouble...'twas the day everything changed."

Helena never thought about her mam as anything but a vile woman, a woman who had left Helena to raise her siblings while she herself had fallen deeper and deeper into the bottle. Had the woman Da described ever really existed?

"What happened? Where did it all go wrong?"

"We'd been at the pub with a few of our friends, tying one on and having a right fine time dancing. You should have seen her, gra. She was beautiful then. Her hair was so dark, so black it almost looked blue sometimes. And, ach, when she'd smile...it was like the whole world warmed up."

She thought back to the last time she'd seen her mam, lying in the hospital bed, covered in burns and calling her a bitch. No matter how hard Helena tried, she couldn't see the beautiful woman Da had described.

"Someone in the bar had started a fight. I didn't have nothin' to do with nothin'." He shook his head as he took a long drink from his steaming tea. "I went to the clink. Thought I'd be out the next day. Ya know, just get a chance to sleep it off, tell my story, and get to walkin' away. But while I was there, someone said they'd seen me stealin' a lorry. Now, I ain't never stolen nothin', not in my whole life. I may do some things others wouldn't understand to get by, but I ain't never resorted to thievin'."

"Why did they get to thinkin' it was you, then?" Helena asked, taking a drink of the bitter tea.

"Because we are who we are. They knew I was a gypsy, and it was easier to use me as a patsy than to wait and actually catch the one who done the stealin'. We're all thieves in the law's eyes."

Unfortunately, Helena knew all too well that he was right. They lived in a world fraught with racism and cruelty. Until they'd come here, they'd seen and experienced the nasty looks and the snide remarks on a daily basis. And not always at major events. Even going to the butcher had been a struggle. No one trusted them. They couldn't enter a shop without being followed around under suspicion of stealing.

"Are you glad we got the shelter of this place?"

Da reached for his back but, as he noticed her watching him, dropped his hand. "Sure, this place gives us some extra security, but it ain't all sunshine and daisies. We gotta fight here just like we gotta fight everywhere. The fightin' here is just a little bit more under wraps, ya know?"

She thought of some of the waiters who still refused

to speak to her. He wasn't wrong to say her family was still plagued by the stigma of their kind.

"But what does it matter? We can't go to changin' nothin'." He shook his head and took a long drink. "We can't really complain. You've been gettin' along right well with the hospital and all. Are you nervous about today's grand opening?"

In truth, she hadn't given the opening much consideration. Every thought had seemed to center on what they had witnessed at the equestrian center, or the state of her relationship with Graham. It seemed like everywhere she looked, there was something she had to work to understand, to fight, to reveal, or conceal.

"Aye…the grand openin'."

"It's goin' to have to be done real careful now that the HG are in town for their rally with their leader, Benjamin Poole," Da said, pouring more water into his drained cup.

"The HG?" She'd heard about the rally, but she'd never heard of the HG.

"They're a vigilante group. Kinda like Red Hand Defenders in the North or the KKK in the States."

Her stomach fell. Of course she knew hate groups existed. There were radicals everywhere in the world, but she'd never been this close to a large group of them, and she wasn't sure if she should be angry or afraid at their presence.

"They hate…*who*?"

"They hate anyone different. Their name says it all. The *Humanity Group*—as in, only humans like them matter." Da came back and sat down across from her at the table. "They're this century's version of the neo-Nazis. White men with blue eyes and an athletic build. Everyone else…" He sighed, not wanting to finish the sentence.

Had the men in the barn been from that group? Was that why they had been spewing hate about her kind?

"Are they against supernaturals?" she asked, trying to control the wave of nausea passing over her.

Da shrugged. "Aye. They're against anyone who they think isn't like them—and supernaturals, they'd be enemy number one."

"Are they here because of the grand openin'? Do ya think the HG knows about us?" Her skin prickled with fear.

The men in the barn had been talking about getting things ready for their plan—had that meant they were planning on sabotaging the hospital's ceremony? Hundreds of supernatural people and their families would be there.

Oh Jaysus, they have to be…

They had to be stopped.

She tried to recall exactly what they had said, but in her memory that time was just a jumble of words and feelings. All she could remember was that they had spoken freely of being responsible for Neill's death, and that they had said something about a staff member. Was the staff member one of their people? Someone from the hospital?

Someone in her inner circle must have been working for the HG. But who? And why? Why would anyone want to join a group that wanted to kill those they deemed different?

She took a long breath and tried to concentrate on the tea rather than the feelings that threatened to overwhelm her.

No one was safe. Not when a group of hate-spewing killers was on the loose.

• • •

Graham's mobile rang, pulling him out of his stupor. For hours, all he had been able to do was stare up at the darkened ceiling of his bedroom as he thought about Helena and the men they had seen in the stalls.

Someone wanted her dead. Yet Helena had seemed almost indifferent to the fact. He had offered to stay and stand guard for the night—that was, to sit outside their cottage with the promise that he wouldn't enter unless it was an emergency. But she had declined.

The only thing she seemed consumed with was pushing him away, and he just couldn't understand it.

He had desperately tried to make her see what kind of trouble she and her family were probably in, but she had waved off his concern.

The phone rang again.

He glanced at the screen as he picked it up. It was her.

Maybe she had come to realize that what he had said, and the warnings he had tried to give her, were real and legitimate reasons for him to come back. Even if they weren't going to talk, or try to make sense of the mess their relationship had become.

"Aye?" he asked warily.

"Did ya know about the HG?"

"What about them?" he asked, rubbing the tiredness from his eyes.

"Did ya know who they are?" she asked, her voice frantic with fear.

He stood up and slipped on his clothes. As he looked back at the bed, his thoughts instantly went to the day

Helena had lain on those white sheets, waiting for him to make love to her.

How things could change in the blink of an eye.

"Sure, I know who they are. Why?"

"Apparently they're the ones puttin' on the rally in Adare—it's a *hate* rally. How did ya not know about this?" she asked, an accusatory edge to her voice.

Did he really have to remind her of everything that had been happening over the course of the last few days? It was no wonder he couldn't sleep, let alone follow events in the village. He tried not to be angry; she wasn't upset with him. More than anything, she was likely scared—just as she should have been.

He knew about the HG. Not even a year ago they had taken credit for hanging a somewhat well-known psychic from the Cliffs of Moher. Three years ago, it had been rumored they had been behind a large fire that had killed twenty in a government-run Traveller campsite. In neither instance was a single person prosecuted for the events.

Though it never made the news, it was an acknowledged fact that when it came to Traveller communities, law enforcement often felt it was a waste of resources to investigate anything. When they were called out about it at press conferences, high-ranking officials often hedged their statements by saying things like: "We appreciate the special circumstances of the gypsy and Traveller culture. While we believe in justice, we also understand the special needs and requirements of their society. As such, we allocate resources according to where they will do the most good."

They didn't care what happened to Travellers as long as their problems didn't overflow into the lives of country folk.

Which meant everything the HG took part in was firmly rooted in the world that rested just outside the sphere of his normal life—and outside the police's sight.

That reality kept Helena's kind hobbled.

"What are we gonna do, Graham?"

His mind was groggy from exhaustion, and no matter how hard he tried to concentrate on what needed to be done, it felt like he was attempting to capture raindrops in his open hands.

"I don't know." He slipped on his shoes and made his way downstairs. "But I'll come pick you up, and we'll get some coffee—maybe in town, so we can catch a glimpse of exactly what and who we are dealing with. And then maybe we can come up with something."

"We're dealin' with the men from the stables, Graham. We're dealin' with murderers."

CHAPTER ELEVEN

The ride to Adare was spent in silence. Perhaps it was the early morning hour and the way everything around them seemed to still have the residue of sleep smeared over it, or perhaps it was the events of the last few days, but every time Helena tried to start a conversation with Graham, he barely spoke.

She couldn't blame him, though. Not really. Not after what she had done to him, what she had said.

Looking over at him, she saw his dark brown eyes were shrouded in shadows, and the thin lines around his lips seemed deeper, as if he had grown older overnight. She had done that to him. She had broken his heart.

Didn't he understand he had broken hers as well? It wasn't that she didn't love him, or that she didn't care—her love was the reason she'd had to break up with him. She needed to protect him.

The old adage came to her mind that sometimes, when you loved something, you had to set it free.

Yet, what if they didn't really want to be free?

Or what if he did? What if he just didn't know how to deal with her now that they weren't an *us*? A little prick of hurt rose inside of her, but she quickly squashed the feeling. She had no right to feel hurt.

"Do you think we'll be able to find the men from the stables?" she asked, in an effort to fill the tense silence between them.

"They can't be too far away, or too well hidden. As long as we talk to the right people, I'm sure we can at least narrow down the possibilities."

"Did you call Giorgio? Maybe he can help us." She knew she was grasping at straws. Giorgio hadn't seen the men, but they had to do something…anything that would help them keep others from being hurt.

"I did. He's looking into the hospital for us, seeing if he can follow up on the nurses who didn't have alibis for their whereabouts on the day of Neill's murder. Right now, it sounds like there are three possibilities—a nurse who works in the med surg unit, and two from rehab. He said he was leaning toward the med surg nurse, a man named Blane."

"Blane?" She remembered the man she had hired. He had come from Northern Ireland and been working in the medical field for the last ten years. He had seemed intelligent, well-spoken, and ambitious—even asking if there was a leadership position that he could apply for. Had it all been because he had been hired by the HG to infiltrate their hospital? Had it all been a show?

Nothing about the man had put her off, but that didn't mean she, and the others seated on the board for the interview, hadn't made a mistake.

"Why does he think it's Blane?"

Graham shrugged. "He's been looking into each of the nurses' lives. Blane was involved in ALF when he was in college."

ALF was an antagonistic group working for animal rights and environmental protection. They were known for infiltrating organizations with known questionable practices or inhumane treatment of animals, in some cases even bombing the buildings and headquarters after they had saved the creatures.

The organization certainly used the same tactics as HG. But how could someone who spent their days helping others, guiding them through the terror of injury and health issues, also want to hurt someone—or kill them? It seemed against the nature of a nurse to act in that way—especially a nurse like Blane, who'd seemed, above all other things, kind.

Humans were crazy. No matter how hard she tried to understand them, she would never be able to truly understand the why and how of how they worked.

Heck, maybe Graham was wondering the same thing about her—how, if they cared for one another, she could want to push him away.

He pulled the car to a stop in front of a small coffee shop just down the road from Barbara's Books, her favorite bookshop. Anytime she'd been lost, she'd always found her way to that place and sought comfort in the pages of a novel. It had been her escape.

She turned to ask Graham if he'd like to go to the bookstore after coffee, but he was already out of the car and closing the door. Had he really wanted to escape their close quarters so badly that he'd nearly jumped out?

He must hate her right now.

Maybe she was crazy to think she should stay. She loved healing, but often it was only the afflictions of the body she seemed to really be able to fix. Injuries of the heart and the head—well, those were entirely different things. And most who came to the hospital weren't there for injuries to their bodies.

Graham walked around and opened the door of the car. He held out his hand to help her out. As their fingers touched, she felt the warm buzz of electricity that had always seemed to come at the beginning of their relationship. Had some of their old attraction returned? Or did it have to do with the science of their bodies? Now that they weren't as directly connected, were their bodies trying to pull them back together? Or was the feeling of electricity a warning that they should stay apart?

She stood up and stepped onto the path, letting go of his hand. "Thanks," she said, smoothing the skirt of her polka-dotted dress.

"You look nice today," he said, motioning toward her.

"Ach, thanks," she said, with a dismissive wave.

Normally she was the type to just wear jeans and a pullover, but she had been feeling down, and she found that sometimes the best way to start feeling better was by looking good. Deep down, though, she couldn't deny that perhaps part of the reason for the dress was to remind Graham of how beautiful she could be.

It didn't make any sense that she'd want to attract the man she'd broken up with, but so much of her just wasn't ready to say goodbye.

They walked into the coffee shop in awkward silence. She opened and closed her hands, trying to rid herself of the numbness that had come after he let her go.

"'Ello," a stout woman with white hair called from the kitchen. "Top o' the morning to ye. I'll be along in two shakes of a lamb's tail. So make yourselves comfy."

"And the rest of the day to yourself," Graham said, returning the greeting.

Helena smiled at the woman's enthusiasm. It felt good to be around someone who seemed free and unweighted by the world. She led the way to a table by the window, a place where they could look out onto the street and wouldn't be forced to stare at one another.

The menu was simple, either a fry-up or oatmeal and toast. She skimmed the menu, but she wasn't hungry, especially not once Graham's knee grazed hers, sending another buzz of electricity up to her core.

The white-haired woman made her way toward them with two mugs and a pot of coffee. "Fine mornin', ain't it?" she asked, motioning to the gray, overcast sky outside. "At least we ain't gettin' buckets."

Graham gave her a polite smile. "It is. Been busy this morn'?"

The woman glanced around the empty shop as if in answer. "It'll get there. Lots of people on holiday comin' and goin'. You must be goin' back up at the manor."

"Aye, it's been right busy the last few days," Graham said in a noncommittal way.

The woman sat the mugs down on the table and filled each of them without asking whether or not they wanted coffee. "There've been some strange folks comin' through here. Say they be comin' your way. What kind of things are you doin'?"

"What do ya mean?" Helena asked, maybe a touch too excitedly, and Graham sent her a look.

The woman gave a light smile and shrugged. "Well, 'twas one guy...he kept askin' me if I was excited about the change." The woman fanned her face like she was having a hot flash. "I didn't have the heart to tell him I went through *the change* decades ago."

Helena laughed, and the sound filled the small shop. Graham's cheeks took on a light blush that made him look handsome in the thin morning light streaming through the windows.

"Now, I ain't assumin' he was talkin' 'bout my bits and bobbles. Do you know why he was talkin' 'bout *the change*?" she asked, putting air quotes around the words.

Graham shook his head. "Nah, ma'am. I dunno."

"Ain't it a little late for you all to be busy up at the manor? It ain't the holiday season anymore. Or does this have to do with the rally that's been going on in town? Have you seen the kind of men and women that thing is attractin'? It's like a swarm of blowflies."

"You had any other run-ins with them? Or have they been good customers?" Graham asked, carefully avoiding the woman's prying questions.

"Ach, they've been fine. Just fine. It's always good to be busy. Mostly they keep themselves to themselves." She looked up like she was trying to catch a drifting thought. "Actually, truth be told, most o' the time they seem to stop their chatterin' anytime I come around. They must think I'm some kind of nosy Nellie, ya know." She said it as if people were committing some mortal sin by keeping their business from her.

"I'm sure that ain't what it is," Helena said, putting her hand on the woman's.

"I thought maybe I was making something out of nothin', but ye know people around here—the locals—we ain't nothin' like that. We stick together." Some of her animation returned.

"Have you seen a man around here—balding, gray haired, a little stout?" Graham asked, obviously thinking of the man they had seen last night in the stables.

"Aye, boy, that could be about all the men over forty who come through these doors." She laughed. "Really though, I see that kind of man almost all day, every day. You're gonna have to be a bit more specific."

They could hardly tell her the man might be a murderer involved in the HG.

"He's probably runnin' with another man," Helena offered.

"Again, love, that's how men of a certain age are. They run in packs."

Helena laughed, imagining a group of sixty-something men moving through the street like wild dogs.

"If you want, loves, you're welcome to stay here as long as you like. Maybe you can catch him in today's comings and goings. I'll get you a couple of fry-ups goin'. You must be famished." With that, the woman spun on her heel and moved toward the kitchen as though she couldn't wait to tell the cook that the son of the manor's owner was sitting in the front with a girl.

Helena was sure it would reignite any gossip that had

been lying dormant through the village about Graham and his gypsy—if nothing else, at least the woman had been kind to her.

She and Graham sat in silence for a moment. She wasn't sure exactly what to say, or how to bridge the distance that seemed to be growing between them.

"Is there anything else we need to do for this afternoon's ceremonies?" he asked, finally speaking up.

Of course he would go straight to business.

She shook her head. "Everything's in place for the luncheon. Mary's in charge of the food and the staff has been preppin' for days. It should go off without a hitch." The blood drained from her face. "Ya don't think the HG has infiltrated the manor, do ya?" She leaned in so she could speak without being heard. "Ya don't think they'd poison the food or anything?"

Graham answered with a quick laugh. "You don't really think Mary would let anyone, for a single second, put her reputation in jeopardy, do you? That woman lives for what comes out of those doors."

He was right; Mary was in complete control. Helena thought back to the first day she had met Mary Margaret— the woman had made more than sure that Helena knew her role in the kitchens. Yet, once she'd proven herself, Mary had been kind. She had been Helena's first true ally at the manor, and one of her closest friends, but they hadn't seen much of each other since Helena had buried herself in work at the hospital.

The waitress came out holding two fry-ups. The eggs looked delicious—perfect yellow runniness with a firm white edge. Yet, as hungry as she should have been, Helena couldn't do anything but push beans and bits of egg around her plate with her fork.

"It's going to be okay, Helena," Graham said. "Everything. We'll get through this."

"How? I feel more *afraid* than ever before." She hated saying the word aloud. It made her sound weak and frail.

He pointed out the window. Across the street was the Boar's Head Inn. It was the nicer of the two inns in town. Its front door was made of heavy hardwood, stained dark by centuries of visitors' hands.

"The men from the stables—if they're simply visiting the village, they're probably staying there. If we don't see them come out, we'll go over there and talk to whoever is working the desk and see if we can find anything out."

It was going to go just about as well as it had with the waitress. They had so little to work with. Graham had never seen the man's face, and she'd barely seen him at all.

Graham was picking at his food just as she had been, giving his nervousness away. He must have known their chances as well, but maybe he was right to keep his feelings to himself.

She opened her mouth to speak, but there was a long creak as the front door to the shop opened. Looking up from her steadily cooling eggs, she watched in horror as her da stumbled in and collapsed on the wooden floor.

He looked at her. "Gra…" As the word tumbled from his lips, his knees gave out, and he slumped to the ground.

His blood pooled on the floor as a strangled scream tore from the depths of Helena's soul.

CHAPTER TWELVE

Helena grounded her body, pushing the bad energy and fear out of her system and pulling in the rejuvenating energy of the world. She tried to breathe as electricity poured through her, filling her with what could only be described as the light of the earth—its heat burned and roiled inside of her. Yet, as she opened her eyes and looked down at Da, some of the energy seeped back into the ground.

"Da? Da? Wake up," she begged.

He didn't move.

Placing her fingers to his neck, she checked for a pulse. She found nothing.

"Da, stay with me. Please. Please."

There was nothing else in the world; she was nowhere, and all that existed was Da as she begged for anything that resembled even a sluggish heartbeat.

She placed her hand on his chest, right over his heart, and closed her eyes. She had to heal him. She had to. He was all her family had. He was the only one who could keep what was left of them together.

The energy seeped from her fingers as she closed her eyes and tried to concentrate on her da's needs. There was a deep pain in his core, springing from his back and moving up to his heart.

What had happened to him?

Though she tried to focus on the pain, on wrapping her energy around the injuries in his chest, tears slipped from her eyes and splashed onto her hands.

He needed her. She had to be present. If he was going to have even a chance of surviving, she had to give this everything. She couldn't let her emotions get in the way.

She gasped for air as she tried to control herself.

Graham stepped behind her and put his hands on her shoulders. There was something comforting about his touch and the way his energy drifted into her, filling her with a new, stronger light. Her fingers warmed, almost as though her power had been amplified. The weakest point in the circuit was where her and Da's bodies were touching.

She closed her eyes and pooled her energy around his still heart, massaging and pressing it as she tried to urge the muscle back into motion. At its bottom was a painful orb. Helena didn't know what kind of injury it was, but she forced her energy there, and tried to use it to knit the flesh and cool the pain. Yet, as she worked, something in Da's body seemed to reject the energy, pushing it back just as hard as she tried to push it to the point in his heart where the pain resided.

"Da...Da...please. I've got to...ya need me..." As she pleaded, her mind told her she was speaking to a dead man, yet her heart refused to let her believe there was nothing to be done.

"I need you, Da," she sobbed, giving in to the emotions that boiled over.

For a split second, she felt his heart quiver inside the bubble of energy, but as quickly as it had come, it disappeared—and with its disappearance came a realization that broke her heart.

She had failed.

Da was gone.

• • •

It was a rare thing to watch a world be shattered, and Graham had no idea what to do. The police were working their way through the area, taking statements, and as Helena spoke to them, tears streamed down her face and splashed on the ever-spreading blot of wetness on her dress. Her hair was strewn across her forehead, stuck to her cheeks with Seamus's blood.

Her aura pulsed dark red with agony and stress. He wanted to go to her. He wanted to hold her until the pain left her body. No matter how long it took—weeks, months, years—it didn't matter; he would be there.

A police officer walked over to him. The man was as wide as the gelding from the stables and, by the look of the crooked scar across his cheek, probably just as unpredictable.

"How well did you know the victim?" the officer asked, letting his white shirt and badge introduce him. He offered no platitudes.

"He was an employee of the manor and my…" What did he call Helena now? She was more than an employee and definitely more than just a friend. "He was my girlfriend's father."

The man's eyes widened with poorly disguised curiosity. "Would you say you had an antagonistic relationship with your girlfriend's father? Did you ever have any disagreements?"

Was the man really questioning him? How could he think he was responsible for Seamus's death?

"Of course not. Seamus was my friend."

Then he remembered the fight he and Seamus had once had, but that had been months ago. He held back from telling the officer. Only Graham, Helena, and Seamus really knew about their disagreement, and he didn't want the officer to spend time coming after him when the real killer was on the loose somewhere—a killer who might or might not be involved with the HG.

"Is it true that Mr. O'Driscoll was part of the Traveller community?" the officer asked. His face was pinched with disgust, as though even speaking of the Pavee community left a sour taste on his tongue.

Graham couldn't allow the man's hatred to get in the way. He couldn't allow Seamus's death to go uninvestigated, like so many other Travellers' deaths had before.

"Mr. O'Driscoll was first and foremost a good man. A man who didn't deserve to die. A man whose death deserves to be understood. The culprit must be brought to justice. I'm sure it is in your best interest to keep anything else like this from happening. Am I correct, sir?"

The man suddenly had a need to look at the toes of his

shoes. "In cases like these, with Travellers at the center, we find that our resources can often be better spent elsewhere."

"Better spent?" He hated nothing more than a bigot—especially one who was supposed to stand for a higher moral standard than the general public. "This has nothing to do with his cultural background. This has to do with the fact that an innocent man was killed in a normally peaceful and quiet town—a town that is currently being overrun by a notorious group of racists."

"I didn't see it written anywhere that he was killed by anyone involved in...what group did you say was staying in the village?"

Was the officer really unaware of the criminal elements that currently resided in the town—in the hotel across the street, even?

"The HG. The Humanity Group."

The man nodded, but he didn't seem at all surprised. The bastard was playing some kind of stupid game. Graham wasn't in the mood, not as he looked over to where the coroner was making notes and another officer was taking pictures of the body. Helena was sitting in the same spot she'd been in when Seamus had appeared in the shop, but now her shoulders were shaking as she sobbed.

Seeing her in so much pain only angered him more.

"They killed him," he said bluntly.

"Who is *they?*" the officer asked, looking back at Seamus's body with an unemotional nod of the head, like the man was just another in the long list of dead he'd seen.

No matter what happened, no matter how much death Graham had seen, he promised himself then and there that he would never become that man—totally devoid of emotion in the face of someone else's tragedy.

"They. The HG. The leaders. They hate Travellers. When you investigate who did this, that's where you should start, and I think you damned well know it, but your bigotry is blinding you to the truth."

The officer crossed his arms over his chest as though shielding himself from Graham's judgment. "Who's the real bigot here, Mr. Kelly? From where I'm standing, you're the one who is filled with hate. Not the men and women of the HG. I've not heard a single thing from their camp that has called for a criminal act—in fact, their rally has been far easier to handle than any Traveller event I've worked."

Graham snorted. "They talk freely about how all Travellers and *others*—" he said the word aware that the officer probably knew nothing of his kind "—should be killed or deported from this country. How is that not hate?"

"I've never heard them talk about *killing* anyone."

"Then you haven't been listening hard enough."

The man laughed, the sound hard and cynical. "If anyone needs to readjust their thinking here, it's you. Have you ever stopped to consider the fact that since you hired gypsies at your manor you have been involved, in no small way, in two suspicious deaths? Don't you think that's a larger red flag than the words of a group that wants to promote social change?"

"I had nothing to do with Chester's death. And nothing to do with Seamus's."

The man answered with a flippant shrug. "I would look at your friends before you start judging others." The man turned, not waiting for a response, and he made his way over to the waitress who had served them their breakfast.

Graham had never wanted to punch an officer of the law before, but there was a first time for everything.

One thing was for sure—they were going to be on their own in trying to find out who was behind Seamus's death.

On the other hand, with Neill's death, the last thing they needed was the cops meddling in their business. They weren't guilty, but if the police learned about the mysterious death...it would mean their necks would be on the line. The law would take no pity on them, not after the officer had made his real feelings known. They didn't need any more trouble.

A thought struck him. If he and Helena knew about the lack of police interest, the HG had to have known as well. And if they knew that the police wouldn't follow up on any wrongdoings, they could kill Travellers and the like at their leisure, without fear of prosecution—or even an investigation. They could kill and run. They could use murder as a diversion. While he and Helena were focused on Seamus's death, they could do as they pleased without fear of anyone interfering—particularly at the hospital.

If he was right, the supernaturals there were in danger— dozens lay in those hospital beds, innocent and unaware of the danger coming for them.

The HG could kill, unimpeded by him, unimpeded by the law.

That was it. They were using this. They were using Seamus to hurt and control them.

Those bastards.

He moved to Helena and put his hand on her lower

back. "Helena, are you okay?" he asked, not wanting to alarm her.

Maybe he had this all wrong, but he had a sickening feeling he was right.

She looked up at him and threw herself into his arms. She wept on his shoulder, her body rattling with deep, hysterical sobs.

"I loved him too. I'm so sorry, Helena." He ran his hand over her hair.

Instead of making her feel better, it was as if his words threw her over the edge, and she made a strange wheezing sound. Her shaking stopped and she leaned back. Her body went rigid and she fell back.

"Home. Take me home." Her eyes rolled up into her head.

"Helena, no…don't. Not here. Not now. They can't see. Don't leave me," he pleaded, watching her fall back into the coma they had fought to pull her from not so very long ago. She couldn't leave him again. Not now. He needed her. They needed each other.

"I need you," he continued to plead. "You're the strong one; if you go, I don't know what I'll do. Please…"

The officer he had been talking to looked at him, brows furrowed.

If the man saw Helena, she would be sent to a regular hospital. They would tuck her away. She wouldn't get the right help. She would be lost to the darkness forever.

"No. Helena. No. Angel, Liam, Gavin—they won't make it out of here without you and your father. Please," he whispered.

He couldn't let them win, and neither could Helena.

Lifting her into his arms, he pressed her face against his neck. "She needs to get out of here. She's exhausted. You can direct your questions to Adare Manor's lawyer."

The officer stood dumbstruck and staring. His mouth opened, but before he could say anything, Graham turned and walked out of the cafe and to his car.

Helena shuddered in his arms. Her eyes rolled back in her head, and her body started to convulse in a seizure. Gently, he pulled her closer, and prayed for her to be okay. He should have laid her on the ground and kept her from biting her tongue, but he couldn't let their enemies see her in this state. They would take advantage of it; word would spread to the HG that they had taken down not only Seamus, but his daughter as well.

CHAPTER THIRTEEN

She stood stuck in that moment in time. Da was lying on the floor, blood pooling around him, and the world spun and darkened, moving out of focus like an old movie. Her field of vision shrank, and her reality was taken over.

Helena tried to push away the gray when she heard Graham pleading for her not to leave. Yet no matter how hard she struggled, the clouds grew thicker, pulling her deeper into the vision. Instead of a moment in the future, the vision centered on Da—the way the blood spread, soaking his salt-and-pepper hair. The wetness was a contrast to his dry skin, the way it cracked at the corners of his lips. Lips that would no longer open and tell her everything would be all right.

Nothing was ever going to be the same.

She had thought life had been hard since coming to the manor, but now everything seemed to come into focus. She had everything she had ever wanted—a wonderful home, family members who supported her, a man who had seemed to love her, and a father who would have done everything in his power to make her dreams come true.

And yet she'd spent her time thinking about what was wrong with her present and what had been right about her past. She had been living in her memories and, for so long, in a world built on the expectations of others. She had been trying to make everyone happy and do the right thing, but she had constantly found herself falling short—and ultimately feeling disappointed.

She should have concentrated on the good things in life. She should have been grateful. More than that, she should have held onto the ones she loved—her da, her sister, and Graham. Yet over the last few months, she had pushed all of them away.

As she stood in the silence of the gray mist, she was met with the sound of hooves and the whinny of a horse in the distance. There was the clatter of what vaguely sounded like bells, but drier, more hollow and wooden. She blinked, the action slow and deliberate, as she tried to recall exactly where she had heard that sound before.

The wooden sound of the bells grew nearer, and with them came a pungent, earthy smell—the scent of death and decay. The Dullahan.

The coach-a-bower pulled to a stop next to her da's body. The phantom driver sat high in the driver's seat with a whip made of a human spine beside him. The driver's rotting head was tucked tightly under his arm. His beady black eyes glanced in her direction, and his putrid mouth opened as if to speak.

In a panic, she searched the ground for anything made of gold—anything that would keep the phantom of death at bay and make it impossible for him to steal their souls. She searched the cafe's tables, but there was nothing.

"No!" she screamed. "No!"

She tried to run to Da, to throw her body atop his and keep them both in this world. Yet, even as she tried, it was as if someone were gluing her feet to the floor with Da's blood. She pulled, and as she moved, she could feel something pressing against her arms...

Fingers. Looking down to where she could sense the touch, though, she saw nothing.

The sensation was strange—otherworldly.

"Ah..." the phantom said. His voice was hollow and as off-putting as his head.

The black horses pulling the coach lifted their heads. Their eyes were bloody, and the liquid dripped down their faces and splattered to the ground, mixing with her father's blood. The horse nearest her stomped, pawing at the ground with nervous energy. The skin on the beast's leg was torn back, flapping downward and covering the hoof with mangled flesh.

The phantom spoke again, but she couldn't make out any words, only an array of sounds that made the hairs rise on her arms.

As the Dullahan spoke, she looked down at Da. A black, inky, oil-like substance spilled from his body and his soul oozed over the floor. The phantom opened the door of the coach with a sickening motion of his skeletal fingers, and the black liquid moved inside.

"No," she said. "You can't have him. I need him. He's got to stay here!"

The Dullahan looked over at her and repeated the

noises that had released her father's soul from his body. There was a pull as the words moved over her, like the sounds were trying to draw out her soul. Before anything could be pulled away, she closed her eyes and concentrated on the energy that pulsed through her and moved up from the earth. As she grounded herself, she felt the pull of the phantom's words lessen, and finally disappear.

The phantom hissed in dismay. "You...you will be mine. No one's soul can escape me."

"I'm not just anyone. *I* control my soul." She pointed at the coach. "Give me my father back. He ain't supposed to die."

The phantom laughed, the sound high and maniacal. "You may think you are powerful, but you have no power over death. Didn't you learn with Neill? When the Fates have a plan, you have no right to alter its course."

"So the Fates killed Neill?"

The phantom laughed again. "You silly woman. Men kill. Not the Fates." He lifted the whip beside him and cracked it against the bones of the horses' rumps. The horses jerked forward, not wanting to be hit again. They started to pull the coach away, but the phantom turned back once more. "I will see you again. And soon, my love. Next time, you may not be so lucky. The Fates may have a plan for you."

The coach pulled away, and as she watched it fade into the mist, she could make out the skulls on its sides, each holding a burning candle. At the back of the coach was a line of femurs; as they banged against each other, they made the hollow, wooden sound, and she wished for a moment she had been right in assuming the sound had come from bells.

The Dullahan disappeared, and the gray mist pulled in tighter around her until there was only her and Da's body. She tried to move; the glue that had seemed to hold her in place loosened, and she moved toward Da.

Kneeling beside him, she ran her hand over his cool forehead and closed his eyes. Da was gone.

She collapsed onto his chest and her body was overtaken by dry, heavy sobs as her heart finished breaking. It was a wonder the Dullahan hadn't taken her; it felt like this kind of pain would be the death of her.

"I'm so sorry, Da." Even as she spoke, she knew the pointlessness of it. She was talking to the body of a man who had once been living. He couldn't hear her.

A fresh wave of tears coursed down her cheeks as she dissolved into sobs again.

"Little woman, don't cry." The voice was small and tinny, like that of a child trying to talk through a can.

She didn't recognize the voice. If it belonged to one of the Dullahan's minions, this time she would let them take her. She couldn't handle any more pain.

She couldn't bring herself to raise her head from Da's motionless chest; rather, she moved just enough to look in the direction of the strange voice.

Standing beside Da's head, his little brown shoes covered in her da's drying and sticky blood, was a small green man. But he wasn't a man. His face was too tight and too tiny to be that of a man, or even a child. The little thing was perhaps only a foot tall, and his fingers were smaller than those of a newborn babe.

The man-thing looked at her and smiled. His teeth were black from neglect, but it didn't stop him from smiling wider. "It's okay, lass." He reached out slowly, like she was a wild animal that would bolt in fear at any sudden movements. "I'm not here to hurt you. Or your da. I promise, lass." His accent was thick with some ancient dialect.

"Who—"

"Am I?" he finished. He looked in the direction of where the Dullahan had faded into the mist of Helena's vision.

"Are ya—"

"With him?" Again, he finished her question.

Could the little man read her mind, or was he just the kind of man who couldn't wait for others?

"The name's Green Thorn. And no, I'm not of his kind. I'm not of his world. In fact, I despise his world. There's nothing I fear more." He shuddered as he spoke, and she could have sworn his green-hued skin turned even greener.

"Ya fear the—"

"Don't say his name. It will call his attention to you. And no, I don't fear him. I fear death."

She could understand his fear. Though, in this moment, she could see death's allure.

"My kind, we don't die. Not in the way your kind does."

"Your kind?"

"You are full of questions, lass. Has anyone ever told you that it is rude to interrupt?"

She sat up from Da's chest and wiped the tears from her cheeks. She was hardly being the rude one, but she held her tongue out of the fear of being reprimanded once again.

He waved her off. "I'm a goblin. We're of the world of the two-spirited."

Her thoughts went to Da's story…the one he'd told them when they'd been children and putting off going to sleep.

"Aye, lass."

"So ya can read—"

"Your mind? Yes." He gave her a smug grin. "It's how I found your father the first time we met. He was always so thoughtful and imaginative. He was so young then. I thought it quite funny he had gotten lost in the mist. There he was, a young Traveller boy—how he ever managed to get himself lost is a mystery. All he had to do was listen to the voice in his heart. Your kind, the Pavee, it's that voice that drives you. But then again, the boy was young and naïve."

She opened her mouth to speak.

"Yes, it's why you're having a hard time in the land of the settled. But sometimes you can listen to that voice. What it tells you will not be the direction in which you are to move your feet, but rather the direction in which you need to move your heart. The voice will never steer you wrong—even if your mind does."

"What am I supposed to do when the voice ain't talkin' to me?"

"Oh, the voice is talking to you, lass. It's just your fear is talking louder. You will find that, throughout life, that will normally be the case. In order to find out what you should do, you must quiet those fears—then the truth will be revealed."

The man walked around to Da's ear and plopped down with his legs crossed. He ran his tiny, bean-sized fingers down Da's face. "It's so sad to lose a man this good. He may have sinned, but he never acted in a way that went against his love of the people he cherished the most."

He ran his finger over Da's eyelashes and pressed at the corners of his eyes.

"What are ya doing?"

Green Thorn sighed. "Your father, he is of the two-spirits. Don't you remember his stories?"

She remembered them, but she'd never thought the fairy tales and the story about the goblin had been true. Even living in a world of supernatural beings, it was hard to believe that the thing sitting beside her da was real.

Reaching out, she poked the goblin's knee with her finger.

"Ouch. Aye, you may be having a vision, but I'm as real as your Dullahan," he said, reaching down and rubbing the place she'd jabbed him. "You didn't have to press so hard. You don't know your own strength."

"Sorry," she said. "I just—"

He waved her off. "I would've thought a lass like you woulda trusted what she was. With gifts like yours, I would've thought you'd been seeing things far more interesting than an old goblin like me."

"Are ya the one who bit my father?"

"Aye," he said with a proud nod.

"Are ya the reason I got the powers I do?"

He shrugged. "Not even I know exactly how one gets your type of powers. I'm sure it didn't hurt that you're of the clutch—the supernatural lineage—but it is the life givers and gods who pick and choose who is gifted. They must have thought you worthy. You should consider yourself lucky, lass. Not many are endowed with gifts as powerful as yours."

She hardly felt powerful. She had failed to save Da, and although she'd healed Neill, the effort had been for naught.

"Your father was well past saving, lass. His heart had quit beating long before he collapsed at your feet. Thanks partly to his powers, he pushed his body past death to see you one more time. His love for you kept him in this world long enough for him to say goodbye. If that doesn't prove the power of love…"

She glanced down at Da and at the bloody hole above his heart. "What—"

"Killed him? Well, that's arguable. One could say it was his own hubris that got him into this mess—or selflessness, or even a quest for justice."

"But who?"

He raised his hands. "I will not interfere with your fate."

"How is tellin' me who was behind my da's death inter-ferin' with my fate? If anything—"

"Lass, if we are given the thing we want most at the moment we want it, the thing is cheapened and devalued. You must struggle in order to experience the feeling of jus-tice that you truly desire."

She was tired of his stupid riddles.

"That was uncalled for. I'm doing nothing more than trying to help you understand your father." The goblin had a hurt look on his face, reminding her of his ability to read minds.

"I'm sorry." She wondered for a moment if everyone who interacted with goblins spent their time constantly apologizing.

"It's why we don't enter your world often. For those not used to our ways, it can be frustrating—and for us as well. We like the fog and privacy. When we are amongst our own kind, we know how to control our thoughts—though I'm not sure such a gift wouldn't better serve your human brethren." He looked at her with a judgmental quirk of his brow.

Reaching down, he put his hands on each side of Da's face, closed his eyes, and whispered something she couldn't hear. Da's body brightened as if it were filled with light.

When she touched others and felt the energy, was that the light that filled her?

The goblin looked up and nodded. "It's the essence of our beings. This is your father's soul." He motioned to the light.

"But the Dullahan," she said, pointing into the gray mist.

"Yes, he took one, but thanks to me, your father was of both that world *and* mine. He was a two-spirit. Part of him will never die. He will be immortal."

Her heart lifted. "He's not dead?" A fresh tear slipped down her cheek.

"Wait, no. His body…this body," the goblin said, motioning toward the shell that lay between them. "It's dead. This is only a vessel. His vessel will be no longer, lass."

A sob escaped her throat as the pain of her loss returned.

"Don't, lass. No tears. Our vessel doesn't make us who we are; it is our soul's journey that is important. Your father, his soul, it will come with me. I will train him, and he will return."

"As what—a goblin?"

Green Thorn laughed. "One is not reincarnated as a goblin—one must be born of our kind. Your father's spirit will roam this plane until he chooses to leave, or he may stay. It's up to him. I've given your father the gift of free will—and eternity."

She took Da's cold hand and stared at his nails. They were turning white from lack of circulation. It felt odd holding death in her hands; this vessel wasn't her father, yet it had once been. "So he's a ghost?"

Green Thorn stood up. He took a bottle out of his pocket, uncorked it, and pressed it to Da's lips. The light that had risen from his body poured into the bottle. As the light twisted out of his body, his limbs became mottled and gray. The hand Helena held turned hard; she let it go, and the stony limb fell to the floor.

Green Thorn capped the bottle and slipped it back into his pocket. "He won't be a ghost, lass. He won't be haunting attics and the dreams of the living. He'll be far more special than that, once I have him trained."

"Will I be able to see him again?" Helena asked, staring down at the stony vessel that no longer looked anything like the man she had known.

"You are of the clutch. As such, he may choose to reveal himself to you when he feels the time is right. Or he may not." Green Thorn sighed. "You would be best served by letting your father go and saying your goodbyes. He may not want to interfere with your life. He may choose to watch from afar, or he may choose not to watch at all—it's a personal choice."

"Why would he make the choice to be truly dead to his family?"

Green Thorn ran his bean-like fingers down his legs and cringed as he looked at the blood that covered his greenish skin. "Living for eternity is not for the faint of heart. It is a painful thing to not only lose your family once—at the time of your vessel's demise—but again when they leave the land of the living. To step back and stay away, it's an act of self-preservation for some. Too much loss can break the soul. And a soul broken—that is a dangerous thing."

A soul broken...

Between all the losses she'd been forced to face over the last year, she could understand Green Thorn's warning. There was nothing more dangerous than a soul that wanted to find those who had wielded the axes of destruction and make them pay.

CHAPTER FOURTEEN

The gray clouds had turned into total blackness, enveloping her. It was so dark that the weight of it pressed against her chest, making it nearly impossible to breathe, and each movement took all of Helena's strength.

There was nothing. No time. No sound. No light. Only the pain of breathing and the piercing needles of fear.

Was this feeling what Da had gone through? Was this what it felt like to die?

It was okay. She was going to be okay. She was just stuck in her vision. In an attempt to collect herself, she concentrated on her breathing, pulling in a slow, agonizing breath and forcing it out at the same rate. This must just be a panic attack.

Or maybe it wasn't. The thought made her breath quicken, and she forced it back.

Panic wouldn't help.

At her tenth breath, a light arose in the distance, red and orange, flickering as it magically grew nearer.

The smell of oily smoke filled her senses, and she could make out the distinct ripple of flames dancing in the darkness, climbing up the side of a stone building. Growing nearer, she saw the small sign at the front of the hospital. The sign's edges were melting, dripping toward the windows of the ancient fortress where flames were licking up in search of fresh oxygen.

Graham ran past, not seeing her as he rushed to the building. "Helena!" he yelled through the open front door, his voice high and flecked with desperation. The doorframe was charred and black. He stopped for a moment and looked at the flames that obscured the door. "Helena!" His eyes were filled with terror.

There was no answer, only the roar of the ravenous fire.

He stepped forward, into the doorway.

"Graham, no!" Helena cried, but her voice couldn't break through the vision. She sprinted toward him. But before she could reach him, he ran into the flames and disappeared.

She stopped as she felt the intensity of the heat. He would never survive. "Graham!" she screamed. "Come back, Graham!"

An explosion ripped through the building. The blast rippled through the air, so powerful that it threw her backward, but she felt no pain.

At the edge of her vision stood a man. His bald head reflected the wicked light of the flames. It was the man from the stables. Beside him was a man with a hooked nose and icy blue eyes. He turned toward her, and she saw that on his arm was a brand—the same as Neill's—and that there was a long, crooked scar across the other side of his face.

The HG had come for them.

She watched in horror as the entrance collapsed in on itself. The stone parapets at the top of the building crumbled and fell to the ground in the chaos. Dust and debris shot out of the door, littering the path with the charred remnants of what had been her and Graham's dream.

There was no way Graham could still be alive.

She fell to the ground, numb.

No. No. No.

This was just a vision. This wasn't reality. Graham wasn't going to die.

She couldn't stand losing another person she loved.

• • •

Graham laid Helena down in her bed in the cottage. Everyone was there: Ayre, Angel, Danny, and Rose.

Angel's eyes were red and swollen with spent tears, but she had pulled herself together after the news of her father's death. Thankfully, Graham's mother had fielded most of her questions and filled her in on exactly what she knew— which didn't include the possible theories about the HG that kept sweeping through his mind.

Angel didn't need to know everything, not yet. Not when Helena required their full attention.

Helena's hair had fallen over her face, making her look as though she had been in a windstorm, and he reached down and pushed the wayward strands from her tanned skin. As he touched her warm face, he felt pulled to her, like she was calling to him from the other side.

"Helena?" he asked.

Her aura was gray—the color it turned when she was deep in a vision—but as he spoke her name he saw a splash of rainbow, as though the sound of his voice had somehow broken through the barriers of her mind.

"Helena?" He tried again, but this time the rainbow didn't appear.

"Is she there?" Ayre asked, coming over and putting her hand on Helena's forehead.

Graham shook his head. "I don't know. I thought I saw something, but now it's gone."

Ayre sighed, the sound coming from deep in her core. For the first time, he noticed the deep lines on her forehead and the way her eyes seemed dark and troubled.

Did she know something that he didn't?

"What's going on, Ayre?"

Ayre looked away from him. "I saw this. I saw her like this. But in my vision…" Ayre stopped, unable or unwilling to finish what she was saying.

"What, Ayre? What happened?" he pressed.

"In my vision, she never woke."

"What do you mean? She won't wake today?"

Ayre shook her head, and tears pooled in her eyes. "No, Graham. In my vision, she couldn't breathe. She suffocated under the weight of her gift. She tried so hard. She's fighting. She is, Graham. But sometimes—" She sobbed.

"You're wrong. You're fecking wrong, Ayre."

Danny put his hand on Graham's shoulder, but Graham moved away as his anger consumed him. Helena wasn't going to die. She couldn't. Not now. Not when he could do something about it.

He turned to his brother. "You have to help her. She helped you."

Danny looked at him with wide eyes. "I don't have the gift of healing. You know that, Graham."

"I don't care if you don't have the gift. She helped you. Now it's your fecking turn. There has to be something we can do." He could hear the desperation and anger in his voice, but he didn't bother to check it. "What about you, Ayre?"

Ayre shook her head. "There's nothing. Nothing my gifts can do. I'm just a seer."

Rose gave a light cough to get their attention. "There may be something. But you're not going to like it."

How could his mother say that?

"If it saves Helena, I'm going to like it," Graham said. "We can't fail her. We have to do whatever it takes."

Rose lifted the bag on her shoulder and set it on the hope chest at the end of Helena's bed. "Don't be upset. If you don't like my idea, we can try something else. But when you told me about what was happening…this was the only thing I could think of that might be useful."

She reached into the khaki-colored bag and pulled out a large book. It was covered in brown vellum, and the symbol of the Holy Trinity was emblazoned in dark red ink on the cover. Rose set the book down on the end of the bed and lovingly ran her fingers over the symbol.

"Is that…" Ayre sucked in a long breath.

"Yes, it's the *Codex Gigas*," Rose said, lifting her fingers and holding them against her chest in reverence. "I…I know it's dangerous."

"Does John know you're here with that thing?" Graham asked.

"I didn't whisper a word. He knows nothing," Rose said, but her eyes were wide with fear.

Ayre stepped closer to look at the book. She reached down to touch it but pulled her hand back, almost as if the book had sent a shock up her arm. "This is more dangerous than you can possibly know."

Rose raised an eyebrow. "I have some idea of the destruction it can cause, but with your help and Danny's, maybe…maybe we can find a way to help her." She motioned to Helena's still body.

"No." Danny sat down in the chair in the corner of the room. He was pale, and a thin sheen of sweat had formed on his brow. "No. I won't have anything to do with that cursed book. No good can come of using it. That thing stole years from me. No. No. I can't." He rocked back and forth, and his gaze never strayed from the book—almost as though merely being in the same room with the object terrified him.

Graham didn't know what to do, but he couldn't let Helena die. He couldn't let her fall victim to her gift.

"Danny, you can go," Graham said, motioning to the hallway. "You don't have to put yourself in danger. Helena would understand."

"Graham," Danny said, standing up, "you can't do this. She wouldn't want us to put ourselves in danger. The spells in that book are fickle. You know the power of the manor grounds. The land is an amplifier. There's no telling what will happen if you open up the portal with this book again. Anything could appear. Demons, ghosts, spirits…think of all the people in the hospital. What will happen to them if you open the portal to the other world and can't close it?"

Logically, what his brother was saying was true. He would be putting many lives at risk if something went wrong, but emotionally he just couldn't listen to Danny's concerns.

"We're not going to open the portal to the other side, Danny. Don't worry," Graham said, trying to quell his brother's fears. "We just need a simple spell, something that can bring her back to us."

"Where do you think she is?" Danny asked, panic flooding his voice. "When you have the forshaw, you already have one foot on the other side. In order to pull her back, you have to widen the portal. She has to be able to wiggle her way out."

"What are you talking about? She isn't dead. She isn't on the other side. Not yet. Not ever." Graham picked up her hand and laced his fingers between hers. Her hand was limp, only making him want her back that much more.

"I know it's gotta be hard to understand, Graham, but Danny's right," Ayre said. "We walk in the realm between the living and the dead; we live in the valley, where there's no time, no spatial plane, only what the vision provides. It's all too easy to make a mistake, to open the portal to death all the way. And it would be all too easy for her to choose to go to the land of the dead."

"Then we have to do this to stop her. To bring her back."

"Any action we take might push her deeper."

"So you're saying that if we don't act, she's going to die. And that if we do act, she's going to die." Graham walked over to the book and placed his hands on its soft leather cover. "Isn't that the definition of damned if you do, damned if you don't?"

Ayre sighed. "It's not that simple."

"Yes," Graham said. "It is that simple. If we do nothing, there's no chance of her surviving. If there's even a small chance this will help her, then we have to do it."

"Her dying ain't the only risk, Graham," Ayre said. "It can change her powers. It can strip her of 'em, or amplify 'em, or change 'em completely. It's a dangerous game you are playin' at."

"Not as dangerous as doing nothing at all."

"If you were her," Rose said, "what would you want us to do? Graham, you know her better than any of us. I think the choice should rest with you and what you think *she'd* want."

His mother's words struck deeper than any of Ayre's. What would Helena want? Would she want to risk amplifying her powers? Would she be willing to lose them? Or would she rather fall into the arms of death than risk opening the portal to the other side?

He ran his hands over his face. Knowing Helena, she would fight the idea of putting others at risk for her benefit. She was so self-sacrificing. She would do anything to keep the ones she loved safe. Yet if he could have spoken to her, maybe he could have talked sense into her and made her understand that he needed her.

What if she became stuck in the purgatory of her mind because they hadn't done anything? The thought terrified him and nullified any of his concerns. To be stuck in limbo—to not know if you were alive or dead or in your own personal hell.

"Danny, is that where you were stuck—in that purgatory realm?" Graham asked.

His brother stared at Helena and chewed on his bottom

lip until little droplets of blood pooled at the corners of his mouth.

"Danny, tell me the truth. Where did you go? Were you stuck in the in-between?"

Danny nodded, and let his lip go. It was raw and speckled with beads of blood. "There were times I was stuck, but other times I went into visions. Visions of my death. Or maybe it was simply me wishing to die. I saw others die. I saw what I thought was the end of the world."

"What stopped you from movin' to the other side?" Ayre asked.

"You mean why didn't I give up and let death take me?" Danny asked, looking toward the woman with the thick dreadlocks. "I knew I couldn't go. I had too much life left to live. I was young, and like you said, there was no time there. It could have been days or hours or years, but I got lost in the nothingness, in the stream of blackness and visions. After a while, it was like that was reality, and everything that had happened before, *that* was purgatory."

"Would you ever want to go back to that place again?" Graham asked.

Danny shook his head. "Between using the *Codex Gigas* or letting me die…today, I'd want to be saved. I'm not ready to die. Not now, anyway."

Rose reached down and opened the book. "I found a spell."

Ayre stared down at the pages of the *Codex*, and her face, normally full of life and color, faded to white. "This, *Manyath's Mwilsha*—Heaven's Trespasses. It will certainly affect her gift."

"But it will pull her back to this world," Graham said,

no longer willing to hear anything against bringing Helena back. "What do you need to make it happen?"

Ayre ran her finger down the list of ingredients, which was inked in ancient Gothic letters and edged with gold leaf. "It's a simple incantation. It will need the blood of one with the gift." She looked at Danny. "And one who is of her kind. Me. And the blood of a lover." She looked at Graham and raised an eyebrow. "Do you love her? Truly and above all others?"

He didn't even have to think about it. "Aye. Does it matter if she doesn't love me?"

Ayre frowned. "You don't think she loves you? Are you daft, lad?"

"We broke up," he said bluntly. "She said she wanted to protect me…" He looked at her and realized the irony. "She wanted to protect me from having to go through something like this ever again. She thought the last vision was because of…you know. *Us*."

"Then it sounds like she loves ya, boy." Ayre gave him a knowing smile. "She wouldn't have wanted to keep ya safe at the cost of her own heart if she didn't."

Self-sacrifice. It was Helena's way. But that didn't change the fact that things had been hard for them. She hadn't said the words to him in so long. Maybe her feelings had changed. It had been months.

"I don't know, Ayre," he said. "If she doesn't love me, will it affect the spell?"

"It might make things a bit off, aye. But I think her love ain't in question in any place but your head."

Rose drew a knife from her bag. "Each of you, as Ayre reads, needs to pierce your skin with this."

"Aye," Ayre said, nodding. "Let the blood drip on the area over Helena's heart." She reached down and opened the buttons of Helena's blouse, revealing the pale skin of her chest.

Not that long ago, Graham had been kissing that skin. Wishing to make love to her. And here they were, just a few days later, trying to save her life.

Ayre read the words on the page and cut a long line across the center of her palm, letting the blood drip upon Helena's unmarred skin. The crimson liquid contrasted sharply with the smooth skin of Helena's chest. As the blood dripped downward, disappearing under her shirt and soaking into the fabric, Helena's breathing deepened, and she took in a lungful of air like someone trying not to drown.

Ayre motioned for Danny to follow suit, and he took the knife and slid it over his palm until rubies of blood dripped onto Helena.

Danny passed him the knife.

Graham pushed the blade into his hand, cutting deeper than necessary—he would give everything if it would bring her back. He let the blood rush from him and fall like refreshing raindrops onto her pale skin. As his blood touched her, Helena's chest rose and fell rapidly and her eyelids fluttered like she was having another seizure, but her eyes remained closed.

He pulled his hand up against his chest, but he didn't feel the pain of the gash, only the agony that came with the need to have her healthy and back in his arms.

CHAPTER FIFTEEN

At the edge of Helena's consciousness, she could hear Graham's voice calling to her.

"I'm here," she called. "I'm here. Don't leave me. I'm here."

But the tempo and cadence of Graham's voice didn't change, almost as if he couldn't hear her.

She could smell the smoky residue of the fire at the hospital, and it reignited her fear. Graham was okay, but for how long? And what about the other people in the hospital?

Graham was there, at the edge of her vision. He was alive. He was with Ayre. He had to be okay. She tried to reassure herself and find the truth of the reality that lay just beyond her reach.

"There's a bomb," she said, trying to call out to them once again.

This time Graham's voice seemed closer, and after a moment, his words became clearer, like a radio that had finally picked up a frequency.

"What? What did she say?"

Helena tried again. "There's a bomb in the hospital."

At the edges of her vision, the light intensified, growing brighter, and she ran toward it.

"I think she said 'bomb,'" a woman, maybe Rose, answered.

"Bomb?" Graham sounded confused. "She's not making any sense."

Helena ran into the blinding white light. It felt hot on her skin, and for a moment she wondered if her mind had played a trick on her, and she was running toward the flames of hell instead of the warmth of reality.

"Look," Graham said. He sounded excited. "Her aura. It's working. Helena. Helena, come back to me."

As he spoke, there was a burning sensation in her chest, like someone had poured boiling liquid on her skin and was letting it sit between her breasts. She reached up, but there was nothing there.

Blinking, she could see Graham, Rose, Danny, and Ayre. They were standing around her room inside the cottage, all staring at a woman lying in her bed. The woman's shirt was open and there was a pool of blood on her chest.

She ran her fingers over her sternum, and as she watched, the woman's arm twitched in the bed. She gasped when she saw the woman's face and realized she was staring at herself.

• • •

Graham reached down and held Helena's hand. It had taken nearly an hour, but as the blood they had spilled on her chest started to dry and the spell they had cast took effect, the rainbow color of Helena's aura had grown brighter and brighter, and at its edges it had turned a brilliant white.

"Helena, open your eyes, my love. Please. I'm here."

Everyone else had gone out to the dining room to get a cup of tea and wait, as there was nothing else they could do. Ayre had assured him all Helena needed now was more time, but the anticipation was agony. What if Helena came back different?

Before, she had acted like a trapped animal, constantly looking for an exit. If she didn't have the gift of clairsentience any longer, would she stay at the manor? Would she even consider remaining at his side?

Graham doubted she would stay now that Seamus was gone. Helena had talked fondly about her memories of travelling as a child, so much so that he doubted she would think twice about leaving if given the option to go on the road with Angel and the boys. It would be Helena's chance to reconnect with her culture and make amends for what she had always called the mistakes of her past.

Would her sister's pull be stronger than the promise of his love?

Would she even want his love?

He gripped her hand tighter and ran his fingertip down the length of each of her fingers. "Helena, I need you," he said, taking advantage of the time alone.

He doubted she could hear him; she hadn't made a sound in the last hour.

"You need to stay at the manor. If you leave, nothing will be the same. No matter how you come back to us, there will always be a place for you here. I want you. I want you to stay. I want…" He closed his eyes and laid his head on the bed as he trailed off, realizing how crazy he probably sounded, begging a woman who was in what was basically a coma to stay by his side.

"Aye?" Helena's voice was hoarse and raspy.

He jerked up, letting go of her hand. "Helena?"

Her eyes were open, and her rainbow aura had returned. She gave him a weak smile. "What else do ya want?" she asked with a light laugh. As she moved, she winced.

"Are you okay? What hurts?" he asked, full of panic.

Helena shook her head. "I'm fine, but my chest," she said, reaching up and running her fingers over the dried, cracking blood.

"We had to…" He wasn't sure exactly how much to tell her, fearing that she wouldn't approve of the choice he had made. "Here, I'll get a cloth." He stood up.

"No. Don't." She reached for him. "We need to go to the hospital. There's a bomb."

"A bomb?"

She nodded. "'Twas in my vision. The HG, they planted a bomb. The grand openin'…What about the ceremonies? Are they over?" She sat up, and immediately moaned and reached up and touched her head, like she'd been taken by a migraine, thanks to the sudden movement.

"Lie back down," he said, reaching behind her and fixing her pillow. "The ceremony hasn't taken place. Not yet." He looked down at his watch. "We have an hour—I do. You have to stay here. We can't risk you having another vision. You've been through enough today."

"I know where the bomb's planted. You have to take me. I gotta keep everyone safe—and you."

"Helena—"

"I know ya want to protect me, but trust me when I say I want to protect ya too."

Though her olive-toned skin was already pale from her ordeal, it seemed to grow even paler as she spoke.

"What exactly did you see, Helena?"

"Visions ain't always right. Let's just hope this one's wrong." She rubbed her temples and slid her legs over the side of the bed. "Help me up. We need to get out of here."

He took her hand and helped her to stand. Her legs were shaky and weak, but she held her body steady out of sheer determination.

"Ayre, Rose, and Danny...we need to grab them. Giorgio is with them now."

"Nah, leave them here. They don't need to be put in—" She stopped before she finished her sentence, and her pause made his apprehension grow.

What exactly had she seen in her vision that she wanted to keep from him?

"Danger?" he asked, wishing for once that instead of being able to see auras, he could read people's minds.

She said nothing. Instead she picked up a pair of shoes by the end of her bed and, with one hand, slipped them on her shaky feet. "Just text Giorgio and tell 'im to meet us at the openin'. We might need 'im."

"Why?"

She looked over at him and put her hand on the door-knob. "Do ya know how to disarm a bomb? I don't, but Giorgio might."

She was right; the former Greek special forces member might not know exactly what to do, but he would have a better shot than either of them, or even both of them put together. Graham nodded and reached for his mobile.

"Wait until we're gone." She slipped out the door and motioned for him to be quiet as he followed her out.

He looked back toward the kitchen, but he couldn't see anyone. He wasn't sure that he agreed with her logic in slipping out without letting the others know what was going on, but, like her, he wanted to keep them safe.

It wasn't a long drive to the hospital. A crowd of the patients' family and friends was already milling about under the white pavilions his staff had set up for the occasion. Nurses were wheeling patients out in wheelchairs and parking them in the shade. Balloons floated lazily in the cool fall air. Everything was just so *normal*, completely at odds with the disaster they were trying to avert.

He pulled the car to a stop.

John stood beside the pavilion's bar, a tumbler of scotch in his hand. He was busy talking to a group of men and didn't seem to notice their arrival.

"I think we ought to be sendin' all these people home," Helena said, motioning to the group that had already started celebrating.

Graham stared at John. One of the men he stood with was smoking a cigar, and the smoke wafted up, catching in the white fabric above their heads like a storm cloud.

"We're never going to be able to convince my stepfather to get everyone to leave. John's glad-handing. He's not going to lose this chance to generate buzz about the manor. This is basically his Christmas. Unless you can convince him that his money's in danger."

"Somethin' far more precious than money is at risk.

Ya—" She gave him a look that made chills move down his spine.

"Is something bad going to happen to me?" A sense of panic filled him. "What did you see? Am I going to die?"

She got out of the car without answering him. He jumped out and ran around to her.

He took her by the arms. "Tell me right now, Helena. Did you see my death?"

She looked anywhere but at him, telling him exactly what he needed to know.

"I don't know what I saw, Graham. We just gotta stop the HG from hurtin' anyone."

He let go of her, numb. Her visions weren't always right, but he couldn't find comfort in the thought this time—not when his death was a possibility.

"Are you okay?" he asked.

"Ach?" She frowned, clearly not realizing that he had already gotten the answer he had been searching for. "I'm...I'm all right. Why?"

"I'm going to die. I know you saw it. Are you okay?"

Her mouth opened, like she was going to speak but couldn't find the right words.

"It's okay, Helena. I...I'm okay with whatever happens as long as I can stop anyone else from getting hurt. Okay?" In truth, he didn't want to die, but if he died for the greater good, he couldn't help but think that perhaps it was meant to be.

With so much talk about the Fates, he wondered if perhaps this was the plan they'd had in place for him all along, from the moment he had first seen Helena O'Driscoll outside Limerick Prison.

His laugh sounded out of place in the dangerously still afternoon.

"I'm not going to let anythin' happen. You're not gonna die. My vision, it was a mistake." She talked quickly, like she was trying to convince herself what she was saying was true.

He didn't buy her lies. She'd had some visions that were wrong, but most had paralleled what came to be.

"Aye, you're right," he said, trying to validate her feelings. He wasn't sure if he should feed her desperate hope, or if he should help her understand that her gift was preparing her for the inevitable, but he went with his gut. "I'm sure I'll be fine."

He leaned in and wrapped her in his arms. If he was going to die, it wasn't going to happen before he got the chance to kiss her one last time.

She met his ravenous kiss with a hunger as voracious as his. She took his lips, pulling the bottom one into her mouth and sucking. He grumbled, the sound something between a moan of pleasure and one of pain—but it wasn't physical pain that made him make the noise. Rather, it was the pain of knowing that he had found something he wanted with every millimeter of his being, and that he might never have another chance at a moment like this.

He reached up and took her face in both of his hands. "Helena—" He wanted to tell her that he loved her, that he wanted every part of her until the end of time, yet he stopped.

It didn't seem right. If he was going to die, he didn't want to weigh her down with his emotions. When he was gone, she needed the freedom to follow her heart—even if that meant falling in love with someone else.

"Aye?" she asked, looking up at him with her beautiful brown eyes.

He would miss those eyes. Her breath caressed his damp lips, making him want all of her.

"Nothing," he said, shaking his head as he tried to convince her. "Just kiss me."

She smiled, and some of the darkness left her eyes as he pulled her face toward him and kissed her lips again. She tasted sweet, like a summer berry, and he wondered how he'd never really noticed that about her before. As he thought back, he realized it wasn't just her lips that tasted that sweet.

His body responded to the thought, growing hard and pressing against his kilt and moving against her belly.

She sucked in a breath through their kiss, probably as she felt him against her. Thankfully their embrace was mostly hidden from view thanks to her open car door and the truck parked next to them.

Glancing over toward the crowd, as if to make sure that no one was paying them any mind, she slipped her hand down the front of his kilt and rubbed it against him, making his breath catch. She let go of his lip and leaned back just far enough that she could speak. He dropped his hands to her hips. She felt so good under his fingertips.

"Next time, there won't be any visions to get in the way," she said, her voice thick with want. She slipped her hand over him, taking hold and stroking him.

"Oh," he moaned. "Oh Jaysus."

It felt so good to have her take control of him, to make him want her so badly, but now wasn't the time or the place.

It was so hard to say no. "Helena..." He leaned his head back, just feeling her hand as it moved over his length. "We...the bomb."

She let go of him, as though for a moment she had also gotten lost. "Aye." Her voice was filled with sadness.

He dropped his hands from her body.

She ran her fingers through her hair and looked down at her chest. "Ach." She pointed at the dried blood from the spell. "I can't be walkin' around like this." Reaching into the car, she grabbed a napkin from the glove box and wiped away the crumbling bits of dried blood.

"You're still beautiful."

She looked up at him with an entrancing smile. She really was the most incredible woman he'd ever known. Everything about her—her strength, her willingness to learn, her ambition, and her passion. She was all he could have ever wanted in a woman.

But as much as he loved her, she could never be his.

A little piece of his heart fell away.

"You're always such a charmer," she said, closing the top buttons of her blouse. As she looked past him, toward the hospital, her smile disappeared. "Did ya text Giorgio and tell him that we needed him?"

He nodded, and he flattened his kilt to cover the residual attraction he was feeling. "He's going to meet us in the hospital in five. Apparently your sister didn't take it well that we just up and disappeared. They were all afraid something bad had happened to you, so I had to tell them a bit about what we were doing."

"They aren't all comin' over here, are they?"

"I told them not to, but they were all supposed to be here for the ceremony. I told them it was dangerous, but you know them. They have their own minds."

"You need to text them and have them all go to the abbey. They need to stay safe. And we're going to have to hurry." She slammed the car door shut and rushed toward the hospital. "No matter what happens, Graham, don't ya be leavin' me. And don't go tryin' to act the hero."

CHAPTER SIXTEEN

The hospital was abuzz with activity. The nurses were help-ing the healthier patients out of their rooms and escorting them to the ceremony. Giorgio stood at full attention beside the nurses' station, and as he saw them approach, he rushed over.

"I told the nurses they are to take all patients, even those who are less than healthy, out of the building." He motioned to the nurse walking by them, who was pushing an elderly man in a wheelchair.

The nurse saw him and gave them a well-practiced smile. "Good luck today, sir. Miss." She gave Helena a salu-tatory bow of the head as she kept walking.

"Aye. Thanks." Graham nodded.

The woman didn't know how much they needed luck.

As the nurse made her way out of the doors, Giorgio turned to them. "Where's the bomb?"

Helena nibbled at the inside of her cheek. "I dunno… exactly."

"What the bloody hell do you mean *you don't know exactly?*" Giorgio's face twitched with anger.

"I just saw what I saw."

"Graham said you knew exactly—"

"I told him that so he wouldn't do somethin' crazy in an attempt to keep me away—to make sure I was safe," she said, sending Graham a guilty look. "I couldn't let him come in here alone, Giorgio." Fear colored her voice.

So that was how it was fated to be. He was going to come into the hospital alone, and then the bomb was going to explode. He tried to quell the terror rising within his chest.

"Aye." Giorgio took a deep breath. "Do you know what kind of bomb it is? Is there a timer? Is it set off by activity or proximity?"

Helena shrugged. "I dunno. I didn't see none of that. All I know is that I saw an explosion. And the hospital collapsed." She glanced over at Graham and shot him the same concerned look she'd been giving him ever since she'd returned to reality.

Giorgio ran his hands over his face in frustration. "I'll start in the mechanical room and move through the basement. Graham, you—"

"He's not leavin' my side," Helena said, not letting Giorgio continue.

He looked over at Graham.

"Aye," Graham said. "We'll work through the first floor. I'll contact you if we find anything."

"I'll do likewise." Giorgio turned and hurried toward the stairs to the lower level.

"Are you even sure it's a bomb?" he asked, waiting until Giorgio was out of earshot.

"There's no question in my mind." She motioned to the staff locker room and led the way toward it to start their search.

"Did you see anything else? Anything that would help us stop them?" he asked, following her toward the room.

There were stacks of blue scrubs lining the walls, each size on a different shelf, and a door near the back led to the adjoining break room.

"Look, I wish I had all the answers," she said, picking through the stacks of clothing near the floor. "But ya know how limited I am. I don't get the answers. I don't get to see the whole scene. I only see bits and pieces. It's up to us to put it together."

He made quick work of the shelf nearest him, finding nothing but more blue scrubs and a set of hemostats. Not for the first time, he wished that he were more gifted—that he could have had an ability that would be of more use than simply reading auras. If only he could walk through walls, be invisible, or be all-powerful. It wasn't that he wanted to be a god; he just longed to be able to fight the forces that seemed to constantly be on the attack.

"What did the men look like who planted the bomb?"

"I only saw the man from the stables. He was with another. They were laughing. And the other one, he had the same brand as Neill."

Graham wasn't surprised a group like that, a hate group, would brand their members like cattle. It was ironic how narrow-mindedness could make a person into a mirror image of the thing they claimed to hate the most.

"Let's take a look in the break room," he said, motioning toward the adjoining space.

Helena stood up and brushed the dust off her knees. "The man who stood next to the bald one had an abnormally long, hooked nose. Blue eyes. He almost looked like a bird. And he had this scar," she said, running her fingers down the side of her face.

She pulled open the door, and through the small opening, Graham saw John. He was talking to a balding, rotund man and both of their backs were turned toward them.

"John, just because you acted, it doesn't change the fact that you compromised our agreement," the balding man said.

Graham recognized the voice of the man from the equestrian center.

What was John doing talking to someone from the HG?

Graham stopped Helena. He shook his head and motioned for her to look into the other room. As she caught a glimpse of the men, her face turned red with anger and she opened the door wider, but Graham stopped her with another shake of his head.

He found some measure of comfort in the fact that these two particular men were standing inside the hospital. If there were any possibility of the HG's bomb going off, their leader wouldn't have been within the hospital's walls.

"Look, you can't let your men complete their mission. I've made amends for the gypsy's father having killed Neill. I never intended for anything like that to happen," John said. "But if you had kept your man in check, he wouldn't have died. At the most basic level, all of this is your fault. You are the ones who broke the treaty. If you hadn't been greedy, wanting more than what I was willing to give, Seamus wouldn't have learned of your plan. He wouldn't have gone after your man."

The bald man laughed. "Don't blame this on us. My man went rogue, just as yours did. This is why you and I have no business working together. We don't need your fleas and freaks."

"Remember, this arrangement benefits you just as much as it benefits me. If you act, you will be forcing my hand, and you can kiss your headquarters goodbye."

The round man laughed, the sound arrogant. "You have no grounds to threaten me. You are one man; we are many. I could have you killed in a matter of hours."

"Don't underestimate me, Benjamin."

The name rang a bell. Benjamin Poole was the notorious leader of the HG. Yet, at the equestrian center, Benjamin had been taking orders from the man in the shadows. Did that mean that Benjamin was the face of the group, but really worked for someone else, someone more powerful?

"It comes down to the fact that we are going to need some sort of recompense. This was to be a major coup for our organization. We've spent tens of thousands of pounds on marketing and pulling new cadets from the rally. It would be a disaster if we were to have done all this work but fail at our mission. We have to stop the supernaturals. They are dangerous. For all we know, they're going to use their powers to take over our country. They're evil—every last one of them."

"You can't honestly believe that. Have you ever even met one with powers?"

Graham couldn't believe his stepfather was actually

standing up for their cause, but then again, how could he not? He had a son and wife the HG wanted to eradicate.

"When I was a child," Benjamin began, "I had a friend who was *a bit off*. He could warm things with his hands. At first I thought it was some kind of party trick. But one day, he and I were playing around at my parents' house. He lost control. The entire place burned—my parents included. And who do you think paid the price? I lost my parents, and no one believed me when I told them about my friend and his mutation. *I* was called the freak. Worse, a *murderer*. I was put into Oberstown Youth Detention Center. He walked free."

"Not all are evil. I'm sure it was an accident," John argued.

The man laughed, the sound low and menacing. "That doesn't make them any less dangerous. Even untrained, they can kill. Can you imagine what they could be capable of if they concentrated their efforts? They have to be stopped. They all have to die. We can't pass up an opportunity to take out the ones within these walls."

"You won't be failing if you choose to leave this group. I promise you that the people within these walls wish you no harm, Benjamin. I can give you something else," John said, with an edge of desperation. "Something I know you want."

"What can you possibly offer me that would be as advantageous as killing these here? What do you think you can give me that I can't get on my own?" the man asked with a sneer.

"What if I can get you the gypsy—the clairvoyant?"

Helena went stiff beside him, and her nostrils flared in

anger. She moved toward the door, but Graham reached out and took her hand, shaking his head in an effort to keep her from charging through the doors and attacking the men.

"I can kill a hundred freaks if I act—that is far better than one," Benjamin said.

"Your chance to kill hundreds is already over. Did you look around on your way in? They are emptying the hospital. Without your guarantee that you will disarm the bomb, I won't have them return. You won't get the chance to act."

The man laughed. "Your argument is feeble. You well know how easy it was to get my people behind your people's lines. If I want something, I'll just take it. Just like I'm going to get what I want with this rally. My group needs a win."

"This isn't going to work, Ben. They're onto you." John readjusted his tie. "Look, I can get you the gypsy by the end of the day. Then you can do what you wish with her. She's more powerful than she realizes. You can keep her, kill her, or *use* her for her powers. It's up to you. But think about all the things you could achieve if you had a woman with you who could see into the future—I mean, look around you. She put this exodus into motion."

"Why would I want to work with one of those *mutants*?" He spat the word.

"Benjamin, you'd be stupid to kill for short-term gain instead of looking at what kind of long-term asset she could be for your organization. Plus, she's smart and a pretty little thing. You could even take her as a wife, or lover."

"Why would I want something like her as a lover?"

John sent the man a wicked smile. "Sometimes the

things we profess to hate are the things we are most afraid of—and there is no better way to conquer your fear than by making it submit."

Benjamin stood in silence for a moment. "What if I'm not happy with her services, or if she refuses me?"

"Like I said," John answered. "It's up to you what you do with her. But if you need to motivate her, I recommend you go after her family. The only thing that gypsy seems to give two shakes about are her siblings and her father before he died."

"That was a smart play of yours. To kill him."

"I wanted to show you that I was serious. That I didn't want you interfering with my business."

What the feck was his stepfather talking about? Had he killed Seamus just to make more money or make up for Neill's death? It didn't make sense.

The door on the far side of the break room opened and Giorgio was shoved inside. "This guy was nosing around," a burly man said, pushing a gun into Giorgio's back. A drop of blood dripped down Giorgio's nose and rolled over his lip; he wiped it from his face with the back of his hand. "Watch out, he's a fighter."

Two other men, both dressed in black, came in and stood guard beside the door of the break room.

"Giorgio? What are you doing?" John asked. "I told you to stay out of things."

"Sir, what you're doing, it's wrong. You should've stayed away from these men."

"And you shouldn't have made the comings and goings at the manor your business, like I told you." John's voice was threatening. "Do you realize the kind of danger that you've put yourself in? And for what? You were one of our best guards."

The burly man who'd pushed Giorgio inside looked toward them, and a smile crossed over his face.

Shite.

Graham let go of the door and grabbed Helena's hand. "Get out of here! Go. They can't get their hands on you."

As he turned to run, the door flew open behind them and a black-suited guard rushed in.

"We have them, Mr. Poole."

Graham pushed Helena toward the opposite door, but as she reached it, it opened, and revealed another man in black.

They were trapped.

CHAPTER SEVENTEEN

"What are you about, John?" Graham asked, pulling at the restraints that held him pinned to the chair at the large wooden table at the center of the break room.

"Don't fight this, Graham," John said, giving him a shake of the head in warning as he motioned toward Benjamin and the men who surrounded him.

Mr. Poole sat at the head of the table, tapping away on his mobile phone, and finally he looked up. "It looks as though we are going to be able to work with your offer, John. We'll take your girl here." He gave Helena a wink that made her skin crawl.

She could only imagine what they had planned for her, but based on the look he was currently giving her, she wouldn't enjoy any of it.

A few days ago, she had thought she had been trapped in her life with Graham. Yet now—sitting here, at the mercy of her enemies—she understood what it meant to be truly trapped.

She glanced over at Graham.

She hadn't been trapped. No, she had always been in love. Maybe it hadn't been all roses and love songs, but she loved him. She'd always loved him. If only she hadn't been a fool and fought it—how different things could have been.

"You can have the gypsy, but I'm going to need my stepson. I wouldn't be able to explain his absence to his mother. Things between us are a bit tense without me surrendering him to your organization."

"Trouble in the henhouse?" Mr. Poole said with a smirk.

Any gobshite who called a woman a hen made Helena instinctively want to punch them. She had been scared, but as the man continued to speak, the fear disappeared and was quickly overtaken by rage.

"You can take him. Get along. I want a little alone time with this fine thing." The man licked his lips like he was trying to taste her on his skin, and the action only enraged her further.

Up until now, she hadn't understood the expression *seeing red*, but looking at him now, with his big, fat, puffed face, red seemed to seep into her field of vision from all sides.

John motioned for Giorgio to take Graham's chair. "Grab him. Let's go. And you and I will talk later about your job."

Giorgio frowned at Mr. Shane, but he didn't say anything; instead, he grabbed the back of Graham's chair and wheeled it toward the door. As he passed by, he leaned down and said, just loud enough for her to hear, "I'll be back. Just hold them off as long as you can."

She gave an almost imperceptible nod.

"Want to share that with everyone?" Mr. Shane spat.

Giorgio turned back to face the man. "I just told her she was going to be getting exactly what she deserved, being a gypsy and all."

She'd always liked Giorgio, but her feelings for him grew. Mr. Shane had him all wrong, especially if he thought he could use him to do harm.

Mr. Shane's lips pulled into a thin, malicious smile as he looked over at her. "I'm sure it comes as no surprise, gypsy girl, but from the moment Graham first talked about bringing you into our lives, I've been against you. The mere thought of you and your dirty, thieving *kind* in my house makes me hang my head in shame. Your kind is nothing but a scourge upon the earth. You are nothing more than tinkerers and thieves. The world would be a better—and safer—place without people like your family."

"I always knew ya were half a bubble off true, but now I know for sure. Take a look around, ya pompous eejit," she seethed. "It is you and your entitled, self-absorbed, elitist chancers who are the problem. You can all be bought for the right price. The same can't be said of my kind. We care about our families, our people, and staying connected to our culture."

Graham looked over at her and shook his head, reminding her of exactly how precarious their position was. They could be killed in an instant, but she didn't care. If they were going to be killed, she wanted to go out after saying her piece.

Mr. Poole laughed. This time the sound came from his belly, like he actually thought she was trying to be funny.

"Do ya thinkin' I'm puttin' ya on?" she continued. "If

ya think you're going to lay one of your pudgy, manky fingers on me I'll stick it so far up your—"

"You have spirit; I'll give you that. But you would be wise, Helena, to shut your mouth," Mr. Poole said. His words were laced with explosive potential so strong that she bit her tongue to keep herself from speaking. "Do you understand, girl?"

The word "girl," and the way the man said it, reminded her of her mam. She didn't think it was possible for the man to make her hate him more than she already did, but once again he surprised her.

She opened her mouth to speak, but Graham spoke first. "Aye, she understands." He pulled against the restraints that tied his wrists to the black plastic armrests. "And you better fecking understand that if anything happens to her, I will make it my mission to track down every member of the HG and personally slit each of their throats. I'll save you for last, and when I get to you, I will cut off your bollocks and feed them to you one at a time, so help me Jaysus."

"Get him out of here," Mr. Shane ordered Giorgio.

Giorgio pushed him from the room, but before the door slipped closed, Mr. Poole called after them, "Idle threats from an idle boy. If you weren't so daft, you would learn how to handle yourself like a man by watching your stepfather."

The door shut, but she caught a glimpse of Graham's face, red, sweating, and enraged.

"Why don't you go with your son?" Mr. Poole said, pointing after them. "And let him know that I'm not one for threats. Those who say things like that to me have a very short shelf life."

"Don't take anything he says right now too seriously. Like you said, he's young and stupid." Mr. Shane rushed after Graham, leaving Helena alone with Mr. Poole.

At least they hadn't tied her down as they had with Graham. They must have thought he would be more likely to fight, but Mr. Poole had sorely underestimated her if he thought she was going to go down without taking a swing at him.

Mr. Poole stood up and gave her his most disgusting smile. "Now, about you, me, and our little arrangement…" He walked around the table and stopped a few feet from where she sat.

She dug her fingers into the chair's armrest so hard she thought her fingernails might pop off.

"Ya can go to hell, ya dirty bastard." She spat at his feet.

"Now, now, you little banshee. You don't have to hate me."

"Yes, I do. I'll always despise small-minded, self-righteous bigots."

"Sometimes the things we must sell to others we don't always feel in our hearts."

"What is that supposed to mean?"

He looked toward the door as if making sure it was closed. "I know you aren't like the rest—you may spit words with the power of hellfire, but I doubt you would have the willpower to hurt. You're too soft. And if you're as smart as John says you are, you'll remember that I'm far better than any thieving little gypsy like you. You will remember your place—or you'll die."

"There are far more non-Travellers than Travellers

who are thieves. You're a right shite to think you're better than me."

"I don't think that I'm better than you. I know it." He leaned against the table and crossed his arms over his chest as he peered down at her. "But that's neither here nor there. I'm here for something more than chatting you up with the advantages and pitfalls of our pasts."

"If you're gonna kill me, I'd appreciate—"

"You're more use to me alive. However, if you choose to continue being cheeky, I may begin to see things differently. I'm sure my followers would love to see a clairvoyant gypsy swing from a tree." He tapped his fingers against his fat arm.

He slithered into the seat next to hers and, reaching over, put his hand on her thigh. "But regardless of what my followers may wish to happen to you, I want to think about the possible benefits you could bring me and my organization. As you may or may not know, I'm trying to open chapters around the world. John was right. Learning more about your people and your kind would be a great asset for us."

"I'm not going to help ya hurt the people I love." She put her hand on her thigh, stopping his fingers from tiptoeing any farther up.

He took her movement as an invitation and took hold of her hand. She tried to pull away, but his hand tightened on hers like a vise.

"I want you…" He stared at her chest, and sucked on his bottom lip. "To willingly join us. But unwillingly may be fine as well."

"Why would I ever do such a stupid thing?" She wiggled her fingers, trying to loosen his grip, but he only held on tighter.

"It's far from stupid. In fact, it's probably the smartest thing you could possibly do. My organization can be a safe haven for you. A war is coming. A war against all supernatural beings. Mr. Shane was smart enough to join our side. You should as well, as there are others, powerful others, who want nothing more than to kill every last one of you."

"If they want me dead, why would I join you, or them?"

"I could promise you, and your family, safety. What we have planned—this hospital, it was only the start. It was going to be the first feather in our cap. Luckily for you, Mr. Shane is a savvy man. A man who knows how to pick his battles—and the winning side."

"What exactly did he do?"

Mr. Poole laughed, and finally, as he leaned back, he let go of her hand. She opened and closed it, trying to let the blood flow back into her fingertips.

"He took a deal to try to stop himself and his manor from becoming the epicenter of the HG's movement."

"What deal?"

"We offered him and his hospital immunity in exchange for the equestrian center. It works well as our regional offices, and we know about the veil."

She shuddered. If they knew about the veil, then they must know far more than he was admitting.

"Why were you going after him and this place if you had a treaty?" she asked, motioning to the room around them.

"It is his fault that we are known. Our agreement stated that the HG were to not be exposed, but then your eejit father, Seamus, killed Neill."

She didn't believe him. She couldn't. Her father was imperfect, but he wouldn't kill a man. Benjamin Poole was a liar.

He looked at her, seeming to wait for a reaction. When she didn't say anything, his face fell slightly.

That must be his thing. He must be the kind of man who got pleasure from bringing others pain. She shouldn't have been surprised.

"As you heard, Mr. Shane thought he'd make amends by killing your father."

"My father didn't kill Neill. He *wouldn't*."

"He knew who Neill was. When he found out we'd planted him so close to you...I think he believed he could get away with it." He reached up and pushed a piece of her hair behind her ear. She moved away from his fingertips, but it didn't stop him, and he drew his finger down her cheek. "I wish none of this had happened, but if anything, it's turned out for the best. Now I have you."

"Ya don't have me." She recoiled from him.

"I heard your father had a bit of a gift for the forshaw as well. Is that true?"

Da had been one of the two-spirits, but how could the man have known? Who had told him about their family and their abilities? What else did Poole know that he wasn't telling her?

"I don't know what my father could or couldn't do."

Poole laughed. "You don't need to keep your cards so close to your chest. Let's just say that I'm a businessman. I don't invest my money or my time into anything until I'm well-versed in its profitability."

Of course he didn't. She glared at him. "If you think

that you can use me, then you haven't done your home-work. I don't care what you want me to do or what empty promises you make. I'll never help you or your group." Her thoughts moved to the bomb. If she didn't help him, would he detonate it? Was he just waiting until they moved all the patients back inside? What if he had made a promise to Mr. Shane that he didn't intend on keeping?

"Think about what you are saying, girl. Think of all the things I can offer you. Think about your family. You need to protect them—whether or not you realize it."

"Where's the bomb, Benjamin?"

He smiled, and the action was far more dangerous than any of the words coming from his mouth.

"It must be nice to see the future," he said.

"The only vision I had was of me killing you. Maybe if ya tell me the truth, I won't have to," she said. "Tell me where I can find the bomb."

"Work with me. Agree, and I will have it disarmed and dropped at your feet as a peace offering. You have my word."

"Tell me where the bomb is."

Mr. Poole laughed. "Sometimes, when you look too hard, you miss what is sitting right in front of you."

She had no idea what he meant, but she was growing tired of the maggot. "You're the scum of the earth."

As the last syllable slipped from her lips he moved to stand and, grabbing her by the arm, jerked her to her feet. He bent her over the table and moved to unbutton his pants before she was even aware of what he was planning.

"I like things that I have to fight for," he said, leaning in until his hot, onion-scented breath washed over the back of her neck.

He held her down with his hand in the middle of her back, but she kicked upward. Her foot connected perfectly with his disgusting body. He groaned and reached for his groin. As he moved, she hurried toward the door. Before she reached it, he grabbed her by the arm.

Heat and energy moved up from her feet and through her body, making her core temperature rise faster and hotter than ever before. It felt as though there were a fire licking up her legs and moving under her skin, but instead of hurting, it made her feel all-powerful and unstoppable.

She reached up and took his face in her hands. His eyes opened wide, and he yelped with pain as the heat from her fingers seared his skin. Blisters formed on his cheeks as the power moved through her and into him.

He tried to speak, but his tongue swelled and filled his mouth, choking him and making his words come out as sputtering, muffled, pained sounds.

Instead of letting go, she pressed her hands harder against his skin, until she could feel the bones of his face underneath her fingertips as his flesh burned away and she watched the life leave his body. She was not soft. When it came to those who wanted to hurt the ones she loved, she was willing to kill.

His skin sizzled under her fingers.

She found comfort in the knowledge that the pain he felt at her hands would be nothing compared to the fiery depths of hell.

CHAPTER EIGHTEEN

"You can't go back in there. It's not safe," Giorgio said, cutting the tape off of Graham's wrists. "Helena's okay."

Graham could hear the lie in the guard's tone.

"What does he have planned? Do you know?" He was so angry at everything. His stepfather. Giorgio. The world. "Why didn't you tell me that you were working with my stepfather?"

Giorgio shook his head. "I wasn't working with him. I was doing my job. And sometimes my job requires discretion. I didn't know until he brought me here exactly what he was up to. I thought he was merely working out some kind of business dealing. I swear, if I'd had a clue he was working with the HG and responsible for Seamus's death, I would have informed you."

Graham believed him. "Everyone has made mistakes here."

Giorgio looked down at the tape around Graham's ankles. "I'm sorry, boss."

"You can't possibly be as sorry as I am. I should never have left Helena in there. We have to go back in and get her."

Giorgio glanced at his watch. "Hopefully she's still in there."

"Do you know anything about what they were planning?" Graham asked, as Giorgio pulled off the rest of the tape and he stood up from the blasted chair.

Giorgio shook his head. "There were careful when they were talking around me."

They made their way around the side of the building. Mr. Shane stood in front of the crowd, giving his obligatory speech to the patients and their families. He touted the virtues of such a place and all the things that it had to offer.

As Mr. Shane spotted them, he motioned Graham over.

Everything rested on this moment. His stepfather cared about nothing more than the manor and the money behind it. Everyone who had come together to raise funds and get this hospital off the ground was sitting there, watching the man who—behind their backs—was supporting a group that wanted to kill the people they were trying to help.

"None of this would have been possible without the heavy lifting done by my stepson, Graham Kelly," Mr. Shane said, motioning him toward the podium. "Let's all give him a round of applause. His unwavering support for this hospital and the folks who work and are treated here has made this place what it is today."

The men and women in the crowd rose to their feet as Graham slowly made his way to the front of the pavilion.

He could expose his stepfather for exactly what he was,

but what would it accomplish? If he told people what Mr. Shane was, it would be the end of their dream—the hospital and everything it stood for would be destroyed.

He and Helena had worked so hard for this. He couldn't let her down.

He couldn't let her stay in Benjamin Poole's grasp.

He turned his back on Mr. Shane and the adoring crowd. He didn't need accolades or applause to do what was right.

He sprinted toward the front doors of the hospital, Giorgio at his side.

"Graham," Mr. Shane said, his stern voice reverberating through the sound system and silencing the applause. "Don't go in there. Don't. Giorgio!"

Giorgio stopped for a moment. Then in one fluid motion, he raised his hand and flipped Mr. Shane the bird. There was a collective gasp from the audience, but Giorgio quickly turned away and followed Graham inside the hospital.

"I've wanted to do that for a long time," Giorgio said with a cynical laugh. "I guess I'm going to need to get my résumé ready."

Graham shook his head as he moved quickly down the empty hallway. "No. You're fine. After this is all over, I am going to get him out. Mr. Shane has no right to run this place or the manor. My mother owns half. If I can get her to see the light about her husband, maybe I can gain control."

"Mr. Shane is never going to go for that."

"I don't give a shite what he thinks. He's going to pay for what he's done."

They stopped at the door that led to the break room.

"Are you really sure you want to take this beast on?" Giorgio asked.

Graham wasn't sure which beast Giorgio was talking about, but it didn't matter. He was going to take down anything and anyone that stood in the way of what and who he wanted—no matter what.

He opened the door. He wasn't prepared for what he saw.

Standing in the center of the room, beside the long meeting table, was Helena. She was covered in a fine layer of gray soot. The chair nearest her looked as though it had melted, and it drooped toward her, its armrests globs of oozing black plastic that reached toward the floor like fingers.

A black scorch mark marred the floor at her feet, and as she stepped toward them, he saw that the ground beneath her was still a perfect white. Almost as though everything around her had been licked with flames, yet she had been left unscathed. Nothing, from her clothing to her soot-covered hair, was tarnished by fire.

Yet in her hands was a blackened skull. On the floor, just to the left of her feet, was a pile of ash. At its center were the curled fingers of a hand. Blue flames rippled over the cracked and overcooked flesh, and Graham could make out white bone where the skin had split.

"Is that...Poole?" he asked, the words coming from him in a whisper.

Helena looked at him and her mouth opened, but nothing came out. Instead she dropped her hands, and the skull she had been holding hit the floor with a dull clatter and rolled to a stop by her feet.

A single tear slipped down her cheek, taking with it the ashes of the man who had once been alive.

"I...I..." she stammered.

"It's fine," Graham said, rushing toward her and pulling her into his arms. "It's fine. You're okay."

"He tried to..."

Graham's gut roiled as he finished her sentence in his mind. "Don't worry. It's okay. He's gone now. You..." He stopped. "How did you do this?"

"You need to get out of here. I told you not to act a hero. I told you," she said, looking up into his eyes. "You're not safe. No one's safe. The bomb. There's still a bomb."

"Did he tell you where it was?" Giorgio asked.

She shook her head, her eyes unblinking. "He only said that it was in plain sight. That we were lookin' too hard."

Graham pulled her tighter against his chest and ran his hand over her hair. As his fingers moved through her long hair, he wondered who exactly he was trying to comfort more. "What's that supposed to mean?"

She shook her head and said nothing, simply letting him touch her.

He leaned down and kissed her forehead. "Don't worry, my love; you're safe. Let's just get you out of here. We can send in a team of guards to investigate. We won't let anyone else in until we've covered every inch of the place."

"Aye, miss." Giorgio opened the door and motioned for them to go. "You need to remain safe."

"What about Angel and the lads?" she asked. "If the HG finds out what happened to Poole, they could be in danger. We can't have them anywhere they can get to them."

Giorgio frowned. "I've been in contact with them.

They're fine; they're at the abbey for now. No one needs to know what happened to Poole—no one *will* know what happened to him. I'll clean up the mess. Neill's grave is still fresh. I can reallocate some things." He led them out of the room and into the deserted hallway.

"They'll know he's missin'. I'm the last person he was with," Helena said, her voice echoing in the still hall. "It won't take them long to pin his death on me."

"They can't pin a death on anyone if they don't know it happened. You just can't admit anything. Act as though you know nothing. In fact, the only person we'll have to worry about is Mr. Shane." Giorgio instinctively glanced toward the front of the hospital, where Mr. Shane was likely still talking to the throngs of people. "You need to go out the back. Make sure no one sees you. Go back to the manor. I'll meet you there as soon as I can." Giorgio moved toward the front and the pavilions where the guests were seated.

Graham took Helena's hand and led her toward the back exit.

"Giorgio and his crew will take care of the bomb. Everything'll be okay. I promise."

She gazed up at him, but her eyes were dark with fear. "Something feels wrong. What if the bomb isn't here, Graham?"

"Don't worry, we'll find it." He tried to ignore the terror that crept through him as he opened the back door and led her outside, into the safety of the open air.

"I dunno, Graham. I just feel *somethin'* is wrong."

"What's going on with you?" he asked, thinking of the burned Mr. Poole and the scorch marks around her feet. "With your gifts?"

She shook her head, her eyes wide with panic. "I don't know. It's like a light switch has been turned on inside me. Everythin' feels different. Like somethin' opened in me, and now I can tap into *more*. I don't know how to explain it."

This had to be because of the spell from the *Codex*, but what exactly had it done to her?

She looked just as she had before her debilitating vision and the spell. If anything, she almost appeared brighter, and the lines around her eyes had faded.

"Are you okay, Helena?"

She glanced down at her hands, opening and closing them as they moved farther from the hospital and closer to the river that would lead them back to the manor. The River Maigue lapped against its banks as it slipped past them, gurgling and splashing on its way toward the sea.

"You know what?" Helena looked in the direction of the sound and smiled. "I haven't felt this good in a long time. It's like...I dunno. I guess it's like I feel complete. Like a piece of me was missin' and now...now I can do anythin'."

"Can you do anything?" The strange, foreboding feeling returned.

She flexed her hands, stretched her arms over her head, and took in a deep breath. "I don't know. But it feels so good."

She'd always been sexy, but now, with her newfound confidence, he couldn't pull his gaze from her.

She knelt at the bank of the river and dipped her fingers into the green water. She motioned him to her side, and he did as she asked. The water was cold, and it numbed his fingers.

Closing her eyes, she whispered something under

her breath. There was a buzzing feeling in the water, and a strange sensation moved up his fingertips and into his arms. It felt like vibrations of music he couldn't hear.

"What are you doing?" he asked.

"I'm callin' on the earth," she said, like it was the most normal thing in the world. "Look." She motioned toward the water with her chin as she smiled.

There, looking up from the water, was a school of salmon. They were all pointed toward her, as if she were their master and they were waiting for her command.

He jerked his hands from the water as a fish bumped against his finger. "What in the bloody hell," he said in a frightened whisper.

She pulled her hands from the river. The fish turned in the water, making ripples as they disappeared back into its depths. "It's fine. Ya don't have to be afraid of me. It's okay."

She sounded like she was truly convinced what she was saying was true, but he couldn't find any comfort in her words. Earlier in the day, she hadn't even been able to control her visions, and now, suddenly, she was like a god.

"You can control animals. Can you control people, too?" He stood up and moved away from her.

She stepped after him and took his hands in hers. "Graham, no one can control people. Not even the gods."

"Is that what you are? A god?"

She laced her fingers through his and pulled his hands to her chest. Her heart thumped hard, mimicking his.

"I'm not a god, Graham. And I don't know what happened, but I've really never felt better." She leaned down and kissed his knuckles. "Ya all gave me a tremendous gift."

Her kiss reminded him of the woman he knew, and

some of his fear and apprehension fell away. She was still in there. She hadn't changed completely. She was still Helena.

"I mean, I'm afraid, too…I don't know what this is gonna mean—these new gifts. I don't even know how I'm doin' it. With Mr. Poole, it was just like the earth knew what I needed. It showed me the way. But only time will tell what I'm capable of."

He nodded as she squeezed his hands.

"What I do know, Graham, is that I need you. For the first time in my life, I feel not just free, but completely empowered. I can do anything. *We* can do anything. With these powers…we can take down the HG." Her eyes gleamed. "We can kill them all."

His fear returned. Had the *Codex*'s dark magic changed her? She'd never been the kind to want to kill.

"Helena, the HG are disgusting, and they need to be stopped, but if we kill without discretion, then we're no better than they are."

"Aye, you're right." She shook her head. "I don't know what I was thinkin'. There's nothing to gain by killin' them like flies. There has to be a better way." She pulled his arms around her. "I'm sorry. I'm just so confused. I feel a bit legless."

He pushed his nose into her hair and breathed in her scent. Her normal, floral aroma was mixed with smoke and the hospital's antiseptic smell. Underneath it all, though, was the power-imbued scent of her.

She looked up into his eyes. "No matter what happens, Graham, I'll never change. I promise. I'll never be anyone but yours. I love you."

"I love you too, Helena."

She took his lips and ran her tongue over his bottom lip.

It wasn't like the kiss they had shared months ago; this was the kiss of a powerful woman—a woman who knew exactly what she wanted. His heart hurt from the intensity of his desire.

Her tongue stroked his, flicking against it and showing him exactly how badly she wanted him. She moaned as his mouth moved against hers, and he swallowed the sound.

He leaned back, breaking their kiss. "I—"

The explosion ripped through the air.

The percussive blast made them drop to the ground.

He moved toward her, covering her with his body as a piece of sod landed on the grass near them. He took her hand and shielded her as they let the world rain down.

CHAPTER NINETEEN

The ground was damp, and as she got up, Helena had to pick bits of wet grass from her dress. Graham was sitting with his knees hugged loosely to his chest. He stared at the ground, dazed.

He looked up at her and frowned. "Why are you smiling?"

She reached up and touched her face. Her lips were pulled up and her cheeks were tight. Why *was* she smiling? She pushed at her face, trying to make the expression disappear, but her body resisted.

What the feck was going on? Why did her body suddenly feel like it belonged to someone else?

She closed her eyes and there was a joy in her heart, a joy she hadn't felt since Da had been alive. As she thought of him, warmth spread through her. Opening her eyes, she half expected to see Da standing in front of her. He felt so close and so real that she had to remind herself he was gone.

Helena reached down to help Graham stand. He

slipped his hand into hers, and where they touched, her skin buzzed with energy. His mouth opened and he stared at their hands.

"What…"

She shrugged. "I don't know how or why, but I think Da is here and he approves." She squeezed his hand, and the buzz intensified.

Graham smiled, but behind it was a look of slight disbelief. Instead of saying anything, though, he followed as she moved toward the manor.

With the silence between them, she noticed the ringing in her ears, no doubt from the percussion of the bomb. Hopefully everyone was okay. As concern worked its way through her, it was dulled by the warmth she attributed to Da.

She glanced back at Graham. His gaze moved over the debris that littered the ground, the bits of torn white canopy, and the metal scraps from the pavilions.

With this much shrapnel, there had to be many injured. Yet in the detritus that littered the ground, she saw no signs of human casualties. There were no wayward shoes or broken eyeglasses. There was nothing directly tied to a person, only the place.

In front of the manor, groups of people were scattered throughout the salvia gardens. The flowers' red heads had faded with the fall, but a few still stood strong, as red as smatterings of blood throughout the grounds.

"Helena!" Giorgio yelled, running toward them from the crowd nearest the fountain of a Hellenistic-style woman. "Are you both okay?" His face was covered with dust and was only clean where rivulets of sweat had cleared away the dirt.

"You're the one who looks the worse for wear. How many were hurt?" Graham asked, motioning toward the surprisingly subdued crowds.

Giorgio shook his head. "So far...there's only one."

Helena glanced around, expecting to see someone on the ground, but there was no one. "Who?"

Giorgio gave Graham a nervous glance. "Your stepfather. He..." Giorgio paused.

"John did what?" Graham said, anger pulsing through his words.

"He...he had a bomb in his jacket."

"What?"

Giorgio nodded, his face grim. "I don't think he knew it was there. He was speaking...and it just *went off*. Luckily the bomb was on the chair behind him—he wasn't wearing it—and no one besides him was close enough to be seriously hurt."

Benjamin had said the bomb was hidden in plain sight. The thought made chills run down Helena's spine. What if Graham had been standing with his stepfather?

"Where is he?" Graham asked.

Giorgio motioned toward the front of the hospital, where there was a bloody handprint on the door.

"Is he going to make it?" Helena asked.

Giorgio shrugged. "I didn't see how bad the damage was, but clearly the HG thought he would be the best weapon. If he had been standing in the middle of the crowd with the jacket on, I'm sure the damage would have been far worse."

Graham sighed. "We got lucky on this one."

"This one?" Helena tried to keep her emotions in check.

He turned to her and squeezed her hand. "You don't think that—even with what happened in there with Poole—the HG are going to stop?"

She stayed silent. He was right. The ache in her gut told her everything she needed to know. Hell was coming.

"We'll search everywhere, from top to bottom," Giorgio said. "I'll call in the rest of our security team members and make sure that there weren't any more bombs planted."

"Get it done." Graham turned toward the hospital. "And make sure these people stay safe." He let go of her hand. "I'm going to go in there and check on John."

From the way he spoke, she couldn't tell whether he wanted to find the man dead or alive.

"I'm comin' with ya," Helena said, moving after him.

"I'll take care of the crowd until my men arrive. Be careful in there," Giorgio said, calling after them.

The strange, warm feeling of Da's presence returned. Was he trying to tell her something? As quickly as she wondered it, the warmth in her vanished, once again making her question her sanity as they made their way into the hospital. If Da had had a message, if he'd wanted her to know something, he would have stayed. He would have given her a clearer sign. Wouldn't he?

There was a loud moan from down the hall, and they rushed in the direction of the sound.

"Get your goddamn hands off me! Get out of here! I'm fine!" Mr. Shane yelled. The shouting continued, the obscenities bouncing off the walls like fat rubber balls.

"I guess he's alive," Graham said with an edge of disappointment. His footsteps slowed.

Inside the hospital room, Mr. Shane stood beside the

bed. His eyes were wild with fear, pain, and anger. He held a stainless steel tray up like a bat, waiting for anyone to come near him. He turned slightly, and Helena could make out the blood dripping down the shredded leg of his suit pants and pooling on the floor.

She was slightly disappointed that he wasn't more injured. He deserved a slow and painful death for what he had done to her, the position he'd put Graham in, and most importantly, the role he had played in Da's death.

"Everyone get out of here." Graham ordered, and the doctor and the nurse scurried from the room.

"You...this is all your fault," Mr. Shane said, looking at Helena with the glare of a feral beast. "You should've never come to this place. You should have stayed back in your caravan, with your cursed family. You ruined everything. You ruined my life. You ruined Graham's."

"I saved your wife. I saved your son. And the fact that I ain't killed ya is as close to sainthood as I'm ever gonna get. The only one responsible for this storm is you, John," Helena said, looking him straight in his crazed eyes.

"You're wrong. You're going to cost us everything. We're going to lose this place—the hospital, the manor, the grounds, all because you and your stupid father couldn't just leave Neill and the rest of us alone." As he spoke of her father, his body started to twitch, and the room warmed with a spiritual presence.

John's eyes rolled back in his head so that only the whites showed. His mouth opened, and his lips pulled tight. On the floor, near the pool of blood, was a collection of surgical instruments. In a series of jerky motions, John bent over, dropped the tray, and picked up a shiny steel scalpel.

"What are you doing?" Graham asked, moving toward him.

Helena reached over and took his arm, stopping him. "Don't. It's not John," she said, staring at the scalpel in the man's hands.

John's body shook violently, and the blade twisted through the air angrily.

"Gra a mo gris?" John's voice was replaced with the familiar sound of her da's.

Da had called her "love of my heart" since the day she'd been born, and hearing those words fall from her enemy's lips made them sound foul. Yet they brought her great comfort, as Da was here. She didn't have to live without him; for a brief moment in time she could have him back.

"Da," she said, her voice cracking. "Is it really you?"

"Aye. I don't got much time, but I couldn't miss my chance to say goodbye, gra."

"Da, I'll never let your death go unpunished. I'll make everyone responsible pay," she said, reaching for him. Then, seeing John's face and his crazed look, she dropped her hand.

"Gra, you and Graham…you don't need the weight of the guilt of killin' my enemies. Ya need to protect yourselves. There are many who're gonna be jealous of the love ya share and the power ya hold." John turned to Graham. "You need to protect her. Aye?"

Graham nodded.

"And you're gonna need to be ready to take control. After today, this place will be yours to run. You're gonna need to find people you can trust. There will be many who wear two faces."

John's body shook violently.

"I love ya, gra…" One eye rolled back into place, and when he spoke next, Da's voice sounded like a garbled mix of his and Mr. Shane's. "Ya have found a good man in your gorger. Love him, gra."

As the last word fell from his lips, Mr. Shane's body contorted and the knife in his hand rose higher.

What was Da doing?

In one swift motion, the scalpel came down. Hard. It pierced the soft skin of John's neck, slipping through his flesh like it was nothing more than tissue paper.

She had once heard that when the jugular was pierced, it spurted blood up to a few feet in the air. Until this moment, she had thought she was just being put on by the telly, but as the blood squirted from John's neck and landed on the ground in front of Graham's feet, she saw that it was anything but a lie.

The color in John's face drained away as the blood pulsed from his body. With each pump of the heart, the fountain of blood grew smaller. John reached up and touched his neck, a look of disbelief on his face.

"No…no. The manor…the money." John collapsed.

His head hit the floor with a sickening thud.

The warmth that came with her father's presence flooded the room, and she could have sworn she felt his embrace. As the sensation disappeared, so did the warmth. They were alone.

Graham stared at the body at their feet. "I always knew I liked your father."

She laughed. The sound echoed through the room, and she clasped her hands over her mouth in horror at her lapse in manners. She hated John. He had killed her father, but she had no right to laugh at Graham's stepfather's death.

Graham walked over and took her hands from her mouth. "Don't feel bad," he said, giving her the look that always made her melt.

"I…" She thought about saying she was sorry for his loss, that she was sorry for what her da had done, but she couldn't lie. She was thankful. The only regret she had was that she hadn't wielded the blade.

"No," Graham said. "John deserved exactly what he got." He pushed her hair out of her face.

"What are we gonna do, Graham?"

He looked into her eyes, and as he stared at her as a sense of calmness wash over her.

"We're going to be free, Helena. Without Mr. Shane, there's no one standing in our way. We can do as we like. We can go anywhere. We can escape the HG's grasp. We can sell this place. We can let others take on the hospital. Helena, we're free, and we're in complete control."

She thought back to the moment she'd stood in the hospital and felt trapped by the world around her. Now, in almost exactly the same location, she felt entirely different.

She would always be a gypsy—always a wanderer with a need to explore, not just her world, but her feelings as well. And now, thanks to her new powers and the man at her side, she had everything she needed to take on the future.

Together and in love, she and Graham held the world in their hands—and if she wanted, she had the power to be its queen.

ACKNOWLEDGMENTS

A huge thank you to the many people who have helped make this book possible. Of course, it wouldn't be complete without a special shout-out to Mary Cummings, Eliza Kirby, Nita Basu, my agents, and the entire Diversion Books team—you are truly remarkable. Thank you all for believing in me and my stories!

This book wouldn't have been possible without the help and contribution of the Irish Traveller community. Thank you for taking the time to answer my questions and for helping me learn about your culture. Whatever errors I have made are due to my own ineptitude and in no way reflect how generous the Traveller community has been in teaching me their lifestyle.

It is my hope this book can be a shining example of the power of one voice...

We mustn't be afraid to fight for what our hearts know is right.

CPSIA information can be obtained
at www.ICGtesting.com
Printed in the USA
BVOW03s0243020917
493792BV00001B/50/P